ROISSY

THE FRENCH LIST

Tiffany Tavernier

ROISSY

TRANSLATED BY
TERESA LAVENDER FAGAN

Seagull
BOOKS

LONDON NEW YORK CALCUTTA

www.bibliofrance.in

The work is published with the support of the
Publication Assistance Programmes of the Institut français

Seagull Books, 2021

First published in French as *Roissy* by Tiffany Tavernier
© Sabine Wespieser éditeur, Paris, 2018

First published in English by Seagull Books, 2021
English translation © Teresa Lavender Fagan, 2021

ISBN   978 0 8574 2 879 0

British Library Cataloguing-in-Publication Data
A catalogue record for this book is available from the British Library.

Typeset by Seagull Books, Calcutta, India
Printed and bound in the USA at Integrated Books International

CONTENTS

CHAPTER 1

The enormity of the world.

Under the vault of Terminal 2E, I'm aware of it every day. Sitting next to me, a passenger opens his laptop. He must be early, because he never looks at the departing-flights screen. A bevy of veiled women passes by. A Russian family wandering around. Six Japanese women, their hair dyed red, come out of the Health and Beauty Shop, weighed down by bags from Sephora, Gucci, Yves Saint Laurent.

'Make sure you have all your luggage with you.'

Not many children. Almost no big groups. The atmosphere is calm this weekday morning. A very elegant Black man weighs and re-weighs his huge suitcase. He can't believe the weight displayed on the scale. Slumped in their seats, some Indians are dozing, their bare feet resting on their suitcases. Some businessmen are talking. Most will fly back and forth in one day. Escalators to my right. I hesitate. I absolutely don't want to miss the arrival of the passengers on AF445 from Rio. The plane has just landed, I still have a few minutes. Opposite Exit 8, a group of China Southern flight attendants go by, laughing out loud. Beyond that there's no one, as if this part of the terminal has been evacuated. The vast dome of the ceiling runs out some dozen metres further. An upside-down shell under which I walk.

The lift doors open, I rush in. Maximum capacity: 26 people, 2,000 kg. Through the windows that look out on to a grey sky, a Sheraton bus drives on the overpass above the terminals. It seems to be flying. I push the button for Arrivals, enjoy the sensation of gliding along, my face glued to the glass. The overpass disappears as it descends. On the lower level, the access ramps become the roof under which tourist buses and private vans are parked. I go up and down three times. The doors open again. A security guard gets in.

'Going up?'

I've never seen this one before. I get out quickly without responding.

At the Espressamente cafe, an American is shouting into his mobile phone that he has no intention of returning and that he is certainly not ready to . . . his voice fades away. He has tears in his eyes. I veer left towards the sixteen glass doors of the 2E Arrivals area. All the doors are covered with an opaque film. Up above, six screens display information for each flight. In the middle, a giant plasma-TV screen is turned on to the LCI News Channel 24/7: flooding in an Asian slum; two men, looking haggard, help a family get into a boat; eleven Egyptian police killed in an attack in Sinai; a cook suspected of eating a dog.

Yesterday, at the same time, there was the surprise victory of a tennis player whose name I didn't hear: a woman had caught my attention. The doors had slid open, she started to run towards a young boy. They were in each other's arms. For a long time . . . without ever kissing, which led me to tell Vlad that it was perhaps her son. Vlad shook his head. He can't understand how I can be interested in such things. *They don't belong to me.* But then nothing belongs to us. An exhausted little girl woke up crying in her mother's arms. A Brazilian couple took her photo. Maybe because of her smocked dress (those dresses, I said to myself, must not exist in Brazil). The couple eventually walked away, the last passengers on the flight following them.

That was yesterday.

Today, two women and a boy are holding up a sign: 'Hooray for Gégé the Most Handsome!' There is also a grandfather with his grandson, a few chauffeurs with their signs, and then that man, in his fifties, a scarf around his neck, whom I'm sure I've seen before. But where? The doors open, the first passenger emerges. She must be around my age, walks forward, looks around for someone. She is tan, not smiling. He isn't there. That's what her eyes say. A group of businessmen jostle her, followed closely by a group of Polish tourists. The flight attendants go by. The tourists scatter.

'The shuttles for the capital, please?'

It's the last passenger, a tall blond guy, twenty-eight–thirty, a Peruvian poncho, backpack covered with 'Save the Planet' stickers. I point him in the direction of the VAL train shuttle. He walks off without taking the time to thank me. A pity, he looked like a nice person, and I would have liked to ask him a bunch of questions: What's the weather like in Brazil? What about the airport there?

In the big waiting area, only he and I are left, the man with the scarf who is now staring at the ground. No one came to meet him, no one else will come. His hands grip the barrier railing, he can't make himself leave. He stays there, not moving, suspending time. The slightest movement and the spell will be broken.

This makes him handsome. Handsome from the waiting that pulls his body towards the impossible.

Soon the flight from Edinburgh will arrive, then the one from Santiago, Chile. I glance at him one last time, hoping to catch his eye. But no, he stands there, motionless. I can only turn back to the LCI images that play in a loop: a shooting killed seven in a high school in the US.

CHAPTER 2

Yesterday, late at night, some wild boars crossed over the runways. Imen (name on the badge), the cleaning woman on T2D, tells me about it while she polishes the huge pot in the green space where a dwarf palm tree is growing. Now she's talking about the wild coast of southern Spain, her homeland, and the exploding number of greenhouses which, for twenty years, have invaded the landscape, turning the land into a huge expanse of blue plastic.

She walks away slowly. A voice in the distance announces the boarding of AF54 for Marrakesh. I settle down on a leather seat, and slowly close my eyes.

On calm days I like to wait for my aeroplanes in this alcove. The flooring on the ground is warm. On each wall there is a large rectangle of ferns. When there is the slightest ray of light, it floods in through the window, lighting everything up.

Three obese passengers go by, laughing. My eyes half-shut, I wonder if they have to buy two tickets each to have enough room.

Later, in T2F, I run into a guy coming back from Burkina Faso, where he's just created an association to help fishermen who are victims of damage caused by hippopotamuses.

'When those satanic beasts get caught in their nets, they almost always destroy them. And back there, a net costs almost 400 euros, an astronomical sum for fishermen who, from one day to the next, can lose their job and find themselves in debt up to their ears! But try to explain that to the besotted tourists who come by the busload to take the beasts' pictures!'

I walk with him to the entrance of the TGV Station. He glances at my suitcase.

'Where are you headed?'

'Me? To . . . Shanghai. I met someone over there. I'm thinking about moving there.'

He shakes my hand warmly, runs down the stairs waving at me. I watch him disappear, my heart beating. I don't know why but the kindness of people overwhelms me.

Outside, I count no fewer than a dozen aeroplane contrails in the sky. A Japan Airlines crew gets out of a minibus. They talk about the terrible weather in Tokyo, and I can't help smiling. Back inside, I glance at the information screen. My flight takes off in over an hour, I have plenty of time. At the Relay store, I finish reading *La Mort d'une héroïne rouge*, and randomly pick up a new novel. *Mma Ramotswe owned a detective agency in Africa, at the foot of Mount Kgale. Here are the things she owned: a tiny, white minivan; two desks; two chairs; a telephone and an old typewriter. There was also a teapot, in which Mma Ramotswe (the only woman private detective in Botswana) prepared red tea. And also three cups: one for her, one for her secretary, and one for the client . . .*

I smile. I'll read this one to the end, too, but not all at once. If the employees are used to travellers who dawdle, they always notice those that stay too long. I walk through the aisles, scanning the article titles on the front of magazines, 'What Do Animals Think About?',

'What If We All Stopped Working?', 'Lose Weight Without Being Hungry' . . . In front of the registers, a couple asks me where to catch the buses for Paris. I watch them holding hands. For a fraction of a second, I would give everything to be them.

THE AIR FRANCE CARD

Every Purchase Brings Your Trip Into Focus

Over the loudspeakers, a woman's voice reminds everyone that smoking is prohibited.

I go down to the Arrivals level, order a coffee from Sarah (badge), close my eyes for a moment, imagine I'm on the streets of Shanghai. A thick cloud of smog covers the city. Gigantic buildings enclose the crowded avenues. It's very hot and humid. I raise my head to catch a bit of sky, I narrowly miss an overloaded cyclist. Then night falls. Quickly. Along the Bund, I contemplate the reflection of the skyscrapers in the black waters of the Huangpu: a soundless liquid galaxy into which I would love to plunge.

In a while, when the final passengers on my flight will have boarded, I'll take the CDGVAL. On sunny days, when the head car comes out of the tunnel, everyone is blinded by the dazzling light. I take advantage to grab the remains of a sandwich or a pizza that tourists very often leave behind on the seats. And one time, I even found a little suitcase containing some children's clothes.

'Where are you headed?'

She must be around fifty, wearing a black trench coat.

'Uh . . . I'm . . . to Manila, and you?'

'Me? To Sydney. I'm paying for my mother's trip as a gift.'

'A nice gift!'

She takes her Air France badge out of her pocket.

7

'Since I've been working here, I'm entitled to four free trips a year with my family. Now, my mother never stops. Last year, she went to Moscow, New York and Dubai! For a woman who'd never set foot in a plane before the age of sixty-two, that's not bad, eh?'

At the PR Long-Term Parking Stop, two AF stewards get on and greet her. I move away a bit, listen to them talk about the boars on the runways last night.

'Eight? But that's a whole family!'

I close my eyes and imagine the herd crossing the runways under the light of the moon. Their shadows opposite the motionless giants.

At the T1 Station, everyone gets out. I hear 'my' AF people talk about a CGT labour meeting that was being held about the problem of personnel reduction. I head towards the restroom, loosen my hair. It's time to choose another destination. Hey, why not Dakar? It seems you can make a killing in textiles, and that there's nothing more beautiful than a sunrise over the Petite Côte in December.

 CHAPTER 3

Today, the sky is sad and cloudy. Outside, the wind is glacial. I adjust the collar of my coat, wrap my head up in my scarf. I walk quickly along the runways. A car approaches, I walk away from the road. If I talk to anyone I'm going to start crying.

It takes me twenty minutes to reach the Concorde. I walk around the little hill on which it reigns, make sure I'm really alone, and seek refuge under one of its wings in the damp, cold grass. Here, there's no sun at all. No sound of birds. Just, in the distance, the rumbling of cars on the A1 highway. I take a pack of cookies out of my pocket, wondering how many drivers leave for work every morning. Millions, probably. For me, it's too late.

Recently, my migraines have been so violent that it seems my head is going to explode again. These days, only the constant movement of crowds can soothe me.

I look up at the Concorde bolted to the ground. I'm sure it would also really like to take off again, relive its glory years when it was king. Its nose pointed slightly upwards, its body stretching towards the sky, it seems to be waiting for the departure signal that no one will ever give again. It doesn't matter; it will wait. Like that man with a scarf in front of the Rio Arrivals door whose eye I tried—and failed—to catch.

I bite into another cookie, stomp my feet to warm them up.

Sometimes, I tell myself that I'd like to stay here my entire life. Anywhere else, the world really scares me. I'm not like them any more. Was I ever? There is so much confusion in me.

A Singapore Airlines plane emerges out of the clouds. It is so close I can even see the passengers' faces in the windows. For a moment, it seems to hesitate before finally touching down. I'd like to stand up, open my mouth and swallow it whole, the plane, its passengers, all their countries, all their dreams.

Vlad would look at me meanly.

'Swallow up an aeroplane? What next?'

Sometimes he wants to slap me.

'I hope you at least bought what I asked you to?'

He can't stand this love I have for aeroplanes. Nor my little 'rituals,' like this one, when I pull up a bunch of grass and rub it against my face until my tears mix with it. A freezing wind grips me, and I jump up. Nothing like a bit of exercise. I'll run all the way back.

IN THE FUTURE, EVEN THE SMALLEST BUSINESS
WILL BE MULTINATIONAL

HSBC BANK—A NEW WORLD IS EMERGING

At the pharmacy in T1, I ask Lucie (badge) for an aspirin and a cup of water. In bad English I tell her I only have foreign money on me. The young woman disappears for a few moments into a back room, and returns with a cup and a pill. An Indian family comes into the store. Their eldest child spilt scalding tea onto his brother's wrist.

Lucie examines the little boy's arm, explains to the parents through gestures that she is going to have to put it under cold water to ease the burn, then apply some cream. The family thanks her, their palms together and their heads bowed. Lucie blushes, she's just doing her job, nothing more. But the mother kisses her hands, apparently telling her husband and eldest to do the same. Their gratitude also overwhelms me.

In front of the Arrivals doors, two men from the Radio France Orchestra are waiting, holding a bouquet, for a group of young Germans who, when they see them, begin singing a lovely canon. When they are done, some Korean women in very high heels applaud wildly and give little cries, and soon everyone is clapping and shouting.

Rémi (badge), who collects luggage carts, tells me about the arrival of a famous singer a year or so ago who, when she caught sight of her lover, began singing an aria from *Carmen*.

'It was unbelievable! The walls shook!'

I stay a bit longer to watch the flow of passengers. I imagine their lives, their professions, invent futures for them which I would like to write down, but, out of superstition, I would never, since writing about them might influence the course of their existence.

Everything is so confused in me. I wouldn't want to cause a disaster for anyone else. My own is enough.

In the afternoon, I witness the reunion of a little boy with his parents. In his grandmother's arms, he stubbornly refuses to kiss them. Taken aback, they tell him that they have a nice gift for him. It doesn't work. The little boy closes his eyes and shakes his head firmly. The grandparents, clearly uncomfortable, try to persuade him. Finally, the father loses his temper. The separation was difficult for him, too. Does he think it's easy to look for work abroad? Obviously fed up, he tries to grab hold of his son, who shrieks and fights back. The mother begs her husband to stop.

'Two months is long. He just needs some time.'

The father gives up, and the five of them walk away. The little boy, more determined than ever, is holding as hard as he can on to his grandmother's hand. The two parents are behind them, their heads lowered.

A Zurich lands, then a Cincinnati. On the loudspeaker, a woman reminds travellers of a special offer: they can enjoy a free sample of desserts at the Grand Comptoir store. There's a crowd, and you have to elbow your way in to reach the table. When I see the little fluorescent-coloured cakes, I hesitate for a moment. Philippe (the chef, badge) holds out an apple-green one to me.

'Taste this one, here!'

I bite into it. His eyes are sparkling.

'So?'

'It's really good, but what's it made of exactly?'

'Matcha tea, it's a Japanese green tea.'

'Did you create the recipe?'

'Yes, and I'm very proud of it.'

A couple of complainers tell me to let them in. Philippe hands me two more samples, winking. In another minute he'll ask for my phone number. When that happens, I pretend I have to leave quickly. What would I talk to a man about? I mean, a man of this world? A man who has a reason to be here, who works here, when I am only a passing shadow?

 CHAPTER 4

Yesterday, I was travelling to Naples, Nairobi and Abidjan, becoming, one after the other, a history prof., a product manager at L'Oréal, the wife of a military expat . . . Wife of an expat, that was a first, and I was brilliant at it. Ah, the boredom of the days spent doing nothing in the big house surrounded by fences, the fear, at night, that men would come and kidnap the children, the difficulty of arranging 'normal' schooling for them, the unbearable heat until the rainy season, the electricity outages, the nonchalance of the help . . .

In T2E, Viviane, an occupational therapist, massaged my hands. A couple of years ago, she was the director of a mid-size retail shop.

'Every four years, they transferred us, fearing that we would become too attached to our teams. I still can't believe I stayed there so long.'

Towards the end of the day, a group of linguists en route to Berlin taught me how to say 'I love you' in Breton, Khmer, Sardinian and Finnish. At night, I fell asleep much more quickly than usual, but in the middle of the night my headache returned. Neither ice water nor a few steps outside helped. Desperate, around 3 a.m., I opened my notebook and tried to write a few words. Instead, I found myself drawing an indescribable scribble.

How many hours did I stay there looking at it?

If Vlad found out, he would force me to get help. To hear myself say what?

PARAFE

A SERVICE THAT ENABLES YOU TO CROSS BORDERS
QUICKLY AND INDEPENDENTLY

At Arrivals this morning, the appearance of a Brazilian movie star caused a stir. Under the flash bulbs of the paparazzi standing on the chairs and tables, her fans descended upon her. Caught unawares, the young woman tried to go in another direction, then a crazy person grabbed her by her hair. Shouting. Movement in the crowd. Cops. Guards. Luckily, I'm not far from the lifts, and I run into the first one that opens.

'What a bunch of lunatics! Are you OK?'

In my panic I didn't even see him. A red badge without a uniform. He holds out his hand to help.

'No, not really . . .'

He offers to accompany me to my boarding gate. I would so like to say yes. Leave everything, take a taxi, open my front door, read the mail that is waiting, water the plants, sit on my sofa, contemplate the view . . .

In front of the 'Quick Cuts' kiosk in T2D, Hadia (badge) is trying to attract customers.

'Extensions, braids, dreadlocks, bangs? For 10 euros, I can work miracles. Are you sure you don't want to?'

She's looking at me.

'I'll bet anything that you're coming from the auction in T3!'

'What auction?'

'You haven't heard? There's supposed to be more than a thousand people over there, and I don't know how many tickets for sale. With the money they make, sick kids see their dreams come true.'

How could I have missed that?

'Fifteen minutes ago, I did a couple of seniors' hair. They had just won a Paris–Haiti ticket. Frankly, I admire them. I could never leave like that without knowing in advance where I'm going. And with a departure within the hour! You should have seen them with their two suitcases. One for a warm climate, the other for a cold! In the room, everyone stood up to applaud them. They were still flushed with excitement.'

An explosion in the sky. Out of the window, a Delta Boeing 767, red, blue-striped wing. Piska (badge), a Black waitress (very tall, very big, too), hands me my coffee. She's complaining about her colleague who is late, doesn't understand why Youssouf, her other colleague, isn't as exasperated as she is. Outside, a pushback tractor is backing up a 777. Tiny figures in orange jumpsuits wave their arms to help the manoeuvre. In the background, a superb A380, looking sad and concentrated, advances slowly towards the runways. As it goes by, humans and vehicles scatter. The control tower has given it the green light, it is a master, both docile and powerful. Soon, I will hear the rumbling of its engines. The buildings will hide it from me until it emerges again, a gigantic whale surging from the water and casting its shadow over the earth. Then, it will disappear into that upper sky which some travellers say is as white and soft as a field of cotton.

'Do you mind if I use this plug? The other one doesn't work, and I need to check my email. My battery's run out.'

'Go ahead.'

'I've just arrived from Kuala Lumpur—how about you?'

'From . . . Lisbon.'

'Wow, that's funny, I'll be there in three days. I sell translation software that's really popular over there. Did you like it?'

'The port, yes . . . at dawn . . .'

I leave 2.30 euros on the table, and take advantage of the argument between Youssouf and Piska to fill my pockets with packets of sugar and ketchup.

When I go down to find Vlad, he shakes his head, exasperated.

'Don't tell me that you went to pay your idiotic homage again?'

'At least someone's still thinking about them.'

'Pff! As if the dead give a shit about homages!'

'It's important to me.'

'The crash was years ago, you didn't even know anyone in it!'

'If you agreed to come, you would understand.'

'Never.'

And yet, every morning, when the Arrivals doors open and passengers from Rio emerge, it is as if *they had all been resuscitated.* For Vlad to understand that, he would have to agree to return to the surface. But he doesn't even want the light of the sun.

CHAPTER 5

The restroom in T2F. This is where I wash my clothes and bathe most often, usually late at night. There aren't any cameras here. Translucid glass basins, glossy water taps, a fabulous counter in fake black marble; a feeling of luxury and well-being throughout. I take off my shoes, walk barefoot on the white tile floor. Radiant.

This morning, no headaches, no cramps, no nightmares. I carried the *New Herald Tribune* (found at dawn in a trash can) folded under my arm, and, like every Monday and Wednesday, like a perfect businesswoman, I got ready to fly to London. In the hall, I enjoyed walking with a purposeful gait. For the occasion, I put on the pleated slacks and ivory-coloured silk blouse that Josias found for me, and the long, navy-blue coat that looks really good on me. I fix my hair in the mirror. It's good, there's no one here, I can go through the purse I've just lifted from the Pomme de Pain restaurant. When I see the 70 euros slipped into the wallet, I stifle a shout of joy. I find an Italian identity card, an international driver's license, a bunch of business cards, two lipsticks, two stamped letters, a perfume spray (Chanel), mints, a mobile phone, keys, three postcards (Istanbul), a photo of two children, a small bottle of water and a roll-on deodorant. I put all of it (except the money) into a plastic bag which this evening I'll slip into the mailbox in T1—steal money, sure, but IDs and souvenirs, never—then stuff the purse into my suitcase. After two months' quarantine—the minimum required for such a find with its beautiful golden-strap buckles—I'll be able to pretend I'm the chic woman I perhaps once was. I turn away from the mirror.

I've never cried like that before . . .

. . . Before I turned up here, everything is a blur. I wake up in a room, unable to remember who I am. Cops are questioning me, but maybe they're doctors. Their shapes in my memory are like shadows that move around me. When I try to talk to them, no sound comes out of my mouth. My head is killing me. After that, I can't remember. It's raining, I'm shivering. Then I land here, where people think I'm a traveller.

That was around eight months ago.

At that time, I was ready to try anything to remember, if only my name, my first name, to find proof that I really did have a life. But instead of memories, only a torrent of light rushed in, too blinding for me to distinguish anything at all. Except, maybe, at times, a few images which could have been real or the products of my imagination.

This blank space in me. My body weighed tons. Each movement hurt. When the pain was too much, I would bang my head against the walls. Sooner or later, the block that was encasing my memory would give way, and everything would become as it was before.

Some mornings I woke up terrified that I had disappeared; on others, I opened my eyes and couldn't understand what I was doing here. I looked at what was around me, I looked at my hands, and suddenly 'my' blank space returned. I felt I'd been buried alive and only now woken up, horrified, realizing there'd been a terrible mistake. But I had to hang on. Some day, my memory would return, my life would make sense again. As for the possible reasons for my amnesia, all the books on the psychology shelf in the Relay store agreed— only a very great emotional shock could have caused it. So, for weeks I tried to imagine the worst. I imagined being raped, tortured or losing my family. But as I would develop these hypotheses, an increasingly vivid impression began to take shape: that instead of being the escapee from one of these scenarios, I was actually the cause of one of them. Why, then, would I struggle to find out what my consciousness, to survive, had decided to erase? Because maybe I had caused a terrible accident, or worse.

In the restroom mirror, new tears begin to flow, uncontrollable, and I begin to detest this face that mocks me with the weight of its guilt. I wash my face four times, rub my arms up to the armpits. Everything is so clean here. So soft. The water, powerful, runs out of the tap into my hands. I feel so good here, letting the crowds move around me. I have three hundred names, as many lives as I desire, so why do I keep insisting on wanting to return to the worst?

The restroom door opens. An Air France flight attendant comes in, wondering why I'm barefoot. I tell her nonchalantly about the Paris–Beijing flight delay, my terrible habit of compensating for stress by stupidly buying things: here, among other purchases, a pair of shoes that are much too small! We start laughing. She's going to Pointe-à-Pitre in less than an hour, a direct flight, returning the day after tomorrow, 'just enough time to take a dip in the pool at the Hotel Continental.' I nod my head. The pool at the Hotel Continental in Pointe-à-Pitre, of course, paradise . . . She leaves, I breathe. Tomorrow, with some of the Italian woman's money, I'm going to treat myself to a scalding bath in one of the airport hotels. For a room at 14 euros per hour, I can certainly afford it. Delighted at the prospect, I turn and look at the jungle-motif wallpaper. I touch it, and I travel there.

Vlad sighs. My stories don't interest him. He doesn't even know why he's still with me. He doesn't say so, but I can feel it. That's my problem, I feel everything. Probably because, like blind people who develop a highly sensitive sense of smell, to fill the space in me, I have developed a rare sensitivity to things of this world.

 CHAPTER 6

How did it begin, and when, exactly? I had to leave. Quickly. I remember the urgency. I said to myself: Let's take this train because this train goes somewhere. In the carriage, the air was frigid. The RER glided along the rails. I said to myself that maybe it would never stop moving. Then I would be saved. Yes, I remember that last word: *saved*, from the despair that was seeping through. Then I fell asleep until a passenger alerted me that we had arrived. Where? I didn't know, but indeed, the train wasn't going any farther.

We were at the end.

The people on the platform headed towards the escalators that, very slowly, took them up to the spider-webbed ceiling, the sight of which was breathtaking: an intertwining of beams reaching up to the sky. So it was up there that I, too, would have to go.

Up there, at the end of the end.

And what a relief it was suddenly to say to myself: great, I've reached the limit beyond which the world is no longer the world. I mean: my world. The city. Its buzzing. The memory of it on my skin. What had been built there, what had been destroyed there. Because, after the end of the line, there are fields here. Fields filled with birds that fly into a sky that I don't know, but the sight of which, every day, reminds me that just one step would be enough to leave everything.

Robocop, Septante, Titi, Moumoune, Georges, Monsieur Éric, Liam, Joséphine, Josias and even Vlad, I'm sure, have had this same thought: the thought, upon running aground here, of having reached that limit when nothing more can happen except a retracing of your steps, or a brief respite, because trying to go further, even just a milli-metre, would mean losing everything.

For them, like for me, this world is our last chance. Leaving it, even if only once, would mean giving up all the voyages, all the identities, in the end, losing the bit of matter we have left, defini-tively breaking the thread that keeps us alive and through whose magic each of us invents ourselves beyond the violence of the world.

SOB

Souls on Board.

The number of people on a flight, including the crew and babies.

 CHAPTER 7

'What can I get you?'

In front of the Hédiard counter in T2F, the young Chinese woman, her hair pulled back, face very pale, scarlet lipstick, looks at me with her big black eyes.

'Nothing at the moment, I'm just looking, thanks.'

Sticks of rock candy, orange strips, boxes of candyfloss. Vlad would be furious at me for spending my money so stupidly. With a Hédiard bag in my hand, who would think I could steal that food left on a table, there, or on a chair, in the time it takes to glance at the display screen or at a text message on a mobile phone? Vlad doesn't steal anything, he waits for me to do the dirty work for him, or for Lucian to offer me a coffee, as sometimes happens here.

'Because here, you have to admit, people are different.'

Even Liam notes it in his journal. As if the proximity of aeroplanes enlarged peoples' hearts.

'Actually, I'd like some candyfloss.'

'Do you want a large box?'

'No, a small one, please.'

'Is it a gift?'

'A gift, yes.'

Chloé-Ming Ting (badge) works irregular hours, which allows her to pursue her law degree. Later, she'll be a judge or a prosecutor.

'Prosecute criminals. I've dreamt of that ever since I was little! Do you want it wrapped?'

'Yes, please.'

EGYPT! *A Dream Cruise on the Nile . . .*

On the moving walkway that takes me to T2C, I open my package, emotions rising.

'The lady is really spoilt!'

Josias! Still as filthy, his hair dishevelled. Neither Joséphine or Liam are with him, he reeks, and I still don't understand why he and his clan haven't been kicked out by the security patrols which, day and night, keep vigil around the airport. The other homeless, yes, regularly, but not them, never, as if they were an exception, or because, facing such a trio, anyone would give up, so clear it is that no mental or physical force could shake their conviction of being 'at home' here. Here: the airport. Their home: the second under-ground level of the T2A parking lot where, since the beginning of the world, they have been sleeping, protected by eleven luggage carts, filled with whatever they have been able to find, forming a barrier around them.

'Spoilt? Not spoilt? Cat's got the young lady's tongue?'

I look at him, worried. What's he playing at? Two Iberia flight attendants come up, ask me if I need any help.

'All's well, thanks.'

Josiah chuckles. I'm feeling more and more uneasy.

'Won't she give me just a bit of her candyfloss?'

I plunge my fingers into the pink sugar-cloud, and give him a mouthful, which he immediately swallows. The two of us have been running into each other two or three times a week for the past six months, but never on the main floor. Often, he takes advantage of these encounters for 'discussions' (something he rarely has the opportunity for with Joséphine and Liam), in exchange for which he gives me food from 'luxury-hotel trash cans,' or confiscated from travellers going to the USA: duck confit, foie gras, bottles of alcohol. Since we met, this is the first time he's approached me in front of everyone. What's the matter with him?

A security guard appears, and I immediately take off. Behind me, I hear Josias boldly asking a traveller for the rest of his canned drink. I think it worked. I don't know, I don't dare turn around.

Three promo photos in a row: a lone house on a deserted island; rows of umbrellas seen from the sky; a man on skis moving away, from the back, in a very beautiful, snow-covered place.

HAVE YOU THOUGHT ABOUT RETIREMENT?

WITH HSBC, THE WORLD OFFERS YOU THE BEST

IT HAS TO GIVE

My heart is beating wildly. I stop, out of breath. Because of Josias, I came very close to getting caught!

'Your passport, please. Last name, first name, date of birth? Are you single? Married? Any children? What is your country of residence? Your address? Do you have another nationality?'

Clinging to the handrail, I force myself to breathe as slowly as possible.

'*Like that, yes, or else your brain won't make it.*'

'*I don't understand, Doctor.*'

Where do those words come from? Outside the windows, cars are moving along on the access ramps, at every moment avoiding the shock that . . . Something suddenly rises up in me, words whose meaning I don't grasp and which, like thousands of bubbles, burst in contact with the air, freeing a deluge of images in which the tops of trees blending with the sky turn faster and faster, bringing with them the windshield of a car that . . .

'Whoa!'

'I . . .'

'Hey, luckily I was there! Did you trip, or what?'

He's holding me with his arm, keeps talking. Inside me, the car windows keep exploding. My body draws circles in the sky.

'I'm going to New York, I'm French-Spanish, I work in the agro-industry, a booming field, what about you?'

Find an answer. Any one. Resist what is breaking within me.

'Marketing . . . A company in Kenya . . . concrete.'

'Ah, yes, I see, Africa!'

Did I have that accident? And if so, when? Where?

'Can you imagine, I travel so much that sometimes I don't even know what country I'm in!'

He laughs again, and looks at me.

'Still, I'd like to experience more moments like these. Unplanned. Over there?'

I hold on to his arm.

'Yes, over there.'

I'm out of breath. He doesn't seem to notice. Invites me to spend a week with him in his gorgeous apartment in central Madrid.

'But you have a choice, I also have a beautiful villa in the South and a flat in Buenos Aires.'

I mumble my thanks. He asks for my address, my mobile number, promising to call when he gets back, because:

'In life, nothing is random.'

He finally leaves me (his phone rings), '*encantado* to have met you.' I stay by myself, dazed. That car dancing in the background? Camera flash.

'Smile!'

A second, then a third flash. I lean against the edge of a seat. But everything is spinning again and it's as if I'm sliding along on a huge toboggan. Over there, in the distance, the light is so white. Is my body still mine, still me? And what is this crowd that is drinking and laughing?

A bride lifts her veil, throws a kiss to a little girl, barely six years old. Delighted, she makes her way through the guests to look at the bouquets of flowers that are floating on the surface of the pool. A hand pulls her out of her daydream, her little sister who wants to play with her. Why did she disobey her? Didn't she tell her to stay with the others?

The little girl starts crying. The older girl leans over her, hugs her tightly. Perhaps too tightly. The little girl cries even more. At a loss, the older girl lets her go. At first, she wants her glued against her, the next thing, out of her sight. Big silent tears roll down the little girl's cheeks. The big girl holds her hand.

'Come on, stop crying, I do want to play with you, but . . .'

'Do you need some help?'

Two flight attendants are looking at me. Those two little girls, the emotions they stir up in me . . .

'There's a clinic here, would you like us to take you?'

'No, thank you.'

'Are you sure you're OK?'

They finally walk away. My heart beating, I lean against the wall. Am I their mother? I suddenly have an urge to throw up, which I must suppress at all costs. Above all, don't attract attention, keep my eyes open, stay standing, as calm as possible. What if I was one of them? The eldest looked so much like me. I touch my stomach in search of an answer. Suddenly everything hurts.

'Is something wrong?'

This time it's a passenger.

'Just a little spell, but I'm much better, thanks.'

He walks away. I slowly straighten up.

BEFORE YOU LEAVE,

LET YOUR TASTE BUDS TAKE OFF!

TROPICANA SMOOTHIE—A 100% FRUIT BREAK

An African family asks me how to get to the TGV Station. I walk along with them for a few steps to put them in the right direction, then sit down next to a group of young girls come to meet their friend who has just returned from India.

'We had a guide with orange hair who showed us all around Agra. He wanted just one thing: for us to be happy! Khajuraho, also fantastic, we visited all the temples, the Indians are really porno! In the bus, a woman, fascinated by my hairslide, tried to pull my hair one by one for three hours. I didn't dare say anything, I didn't want to seem like an asshole Westerner. Varanasi, the dirtiest city I've ever seen. Cow shit everywhere, so much that people cry out "dung" every two metres to warn the people behind them. But that's not all. It's filled with cockroaches, grasshoppers, mosquitoes, garbage and so many dogs that they didn't even consider attacking us. Luckily, there was no sign of cripples or lepers. People are so ignorant, they'll tell you just about anything!'

I stand up, and for a time, follow the lines on the ground that form large diamond shapes.

This hole in me, the tragedy it's holding. Don't stir all that up.

Those little girls . . .

Move. Walk. Run if I must. But don't give into it. Otherwise, absolute night.

★

Here, she doesn't have a real body. But the water that flows over her hands, she does feel that. So she has a body, after all. Or at least skin. Extraordinarily sensitive skin with which, protected by the white that envelops it, she can still enjoy the world, a space where she is weightless and where, as if undecided, her heart is beating. A heart barely formed, yet so full of love, so full of tenderness beyond the cries that surge up in her. Ragged cries that make her scratch herself until she's out of breath. A breath, where, in this bubble, away from all the tragedies, she is walking, with something that tastes like cotton in her mouth; now her world, whose walls are thickening with the passing of time, protecting her evermore from the chasm that awaits her, a gaping mouth which she still manages to feel when it knocks around in her head or when, like yesterday, the memory resurfaces, crazy, and when her nails, in her sleep, without any control, scratch her. Her eyes, which she opens, her eyes like a supplication, her little frantic suitcase that she pulls, that's it, she no longer feels anything at all, not the torment, not the pain, the crowd enters her once again, its clear comings-and-goings. Without a first or last name, again she walks to it. Aberrant, translucid. And it's so much for the better, because her memory contains a secret so heavy that if it were simply to appear everything here might disappear, and how could she want that? She feels so good here. Hold out her hands to the wreckage, demand its return, why?

 CHAPTER 8

In T1, I stop in front of the huge red pine trees dusted with fake snow. An elderly man sighs as he tells me about Bogota, the city where he was born. Everything is changing so quickly there, rents just keep on climbing . . .

'Even hot chocolate, they don't serve it with a piece of cheese any more. But that used to be the custom throughout the country!'

I question Vlad with a look.

'Did you know that?'

'What?'

'That they served hot chocolate with cheese in Colombia?'

'No.'

'In any case, with all these addresses I've been collecting, I could easily do a tour of the planet.'

'Why would you do that?'

'I don't know, to discover the world.'

'The world is the same everywhere. The same smell. The same idiocy.'

'Vlad . . .'

'You still haven't understood that they invite you so they can fuck you?'

'Not necessarily, and anyway, they have the right to try their luck, don't they?'

'And you call that kindness?'

'And what would you call it, when you ask me to do that?'

'You don't understand anything.'

'What makes you think I don't understand anything?'

'I stink, you still talk to me.'

'You don't stink, Vlad.'

'We all stink! Except them, they prefer to run around up there, with their plans for houses, pools, organized trips. As if all that were going to change the course of things!'

He turns his back to me, retreats into his corner. I would really like to tell him about my fear of the resurging memories, the little girls, not knowing if they are my children or if they are still alive, and I curl up next to him, as I sometimes do until his wounded, brutal body takes me. Washing away everything. But now, given his rotten mood, I decide to go back up to the surface for some air.

Night has fallen. I wander, being careful not to seem too fragile. I've had my dose of compassion today. What would have happened if the flight attendants had insisted on taking me to the clinic, or if, sitting next to the Spanish businessman, I had passed out?

At the information booth next to Door 36, a sign announces that there is still time to reserve a cabaret evening. In a corner, two soldiers are tying their boots.

Gradually, the airport empties. In the sky, the ballet of planes is more spaced apart.

Around 11, I go down to the parking lot, making sure no one is following me. I haven't seen Josias since he verbally accosted me in a public space. I would like him to explain himself. The lift doors open. I exit and head to the right towards the space that is accessible through the sliding doors. This is where, surrounded by their eleven carts, they have staked their claim: the place is relatively isolated and it's comfortable here. I advance cautiously. Liam, with his skinny body and wobbly gait, looks like he's going to break apart. Will I end up like that one day? Joséphine, their 'mother,' frightens me, too, when I run into her upstairs with her haggard face, leaning on her cart and sorting through everything obsessively. For her, Liam and Josias are her sons and woe to anyone who dares to approach them.

I am less than a metre from their camp: the piles of clothes, shoes, food containers, cans, broken toys and bric-a-brac accumulated in their carts prevent me from seeing them. It smells of urine, and I'm just about to turn around when Josias, shirtless, appears in front of me, his finger on his lips, gesturing for me to wait for him where we usually meet, at the far end of the parking lot. No one ever goes over there, and we can sit on a little ledge.

Five minutes later, he rushes over, delighted, with half of a three-cheese pizza that he's earned from the Pizza Hut staff in exchange for little tasks.

'Christmas is celebrated, isn't it?'

'Christmas is in ten days.'

'Don't be like that, I have a real scoop: in Nepal, they've made a three-year-old kid a living goddess. Until she reaches puberty, they're going to keep her locked up in a palace, and when she leaves, she has to be carried around by three men so her feet don't touch the impure ground!'

'. . .'

'And in Marseille today, there were traffic jams because of a bus drivers' strike . . .'

'. . .'

'Are you really that mad at me?'

'Do you want them to throw me out?'

'I just wanted to talk to you, that's all.'

'That's all?!'

'Can't you see you're like them?'

'Oh, so they tell you that, too?'

'Like them with some minor differences, OK . . . Fine, I won't do it again. Does that suit you?'

'It suits me if you keep your word.'

'It's so much better when you smile. Sometimes I wonder if you were married, if you had any kids. You're so beautiful.'

'How did you learn that about Nepal?'

'A Hungarian student.'

'Do the Nepalese really believe in the thing about their living goddess?'

'Who gave you the candyfloss?'

'Are you jealous?'

'Jealous doesn't mean I love you.'

'Me, neither, Josias, I don't know much about your life.'

'Maybe, but one day I'll tell you.'

'Why not now?'

'It's almost Christmas.'

'What does that matter?'

'It's not a time to say things. By the way, Liam started writing again. He asked me if I knew anyone who would agree to edit it. I told him I had a well-connected friend in the National Education Department . . .'

'And?'

'OK, National Education, I made that up, but for Liam, you know him, that was enough. What do you say?'

'Me?'

'There's a jackpot in it for you.'

'Does Joséphine know about it?'

'Joséphine is sleeping it off. The jackpot: two cans of foie gras, and a bottle of vodka.'

'With Liam, it's complicated, Josias . . . '

'There's something else . . . something you've probably been dreaming about.'

'Go ahead.'

'A badge lanyard. With that around your neck, all you have to do is stick the end under your scarf to make it look like you have a badge, and all doors will open!'

'You've convinced me—let's do it!'

'I'm not the best?'

'Yes, you are.'

'Then kiss me.'

'No.'

'Just on the lips.'

'No.'

'Shit, don't fool around, I have a huge hard on.'

'No.'

'At least touch it.'

'No.'

'The last time . . . '

'What, the last time?'

'You would have said yes to an aeroplane.'

'To a clean aeroplane, yes.'

LIAM'S NOTEBOOK, 1

(edited)

He's making it through, he's making it through, even though he never went to the Koranic school, but when they find out that he knows, they will kill him and will send him DEAD to the TEN DESTINATIONS AT 1,000 EUROS! Then he won't be able to reveal anything any more!

The G letters really get it, especially the GUESS and the GUCCI that arrive from Mexico, from Caracas, from Las Vegas. They pretend to laugh and say that they went on an 'escapade'. Escapade is the code! The code to say that danger is threatening more and more! They all hide their fear and that's really good because if not the Censor would fall on them and it would be an abomination because it is to them that he must reveal the BIG SECRET or else no one will ever know anything!

He, alone, can do it, because He knows WHOSE son He is and that's why He knows EVERYTHING! Even the Censor doesn't know that He is that one! (The Censor thinks that his FATHER never had children and even the FATHER doesn't know that he has a Son!)

But the Day when he will reveal THE BIG SECRET, then the FATHER will understand EVERYTHING and the Censor will no longer be able to act and EVERYONE will be able to get rid of the Letters that accumulate on their clothes because there will no longer be any reason to be afraid.

TOURISM will be BANNED!

Then THE TEN DESTINATIONS will disappear by themselves. Cities will rediscover their TRUE names. People, too. Everyone will talk to each other WITHOUT A CODE!!!! No one will be burdened by Letters any more. Rolling luggage will no longer heat up the ground. There will be no more flowing, no more travel. EVERYTHING WILL BE SOOTHED. And since, thanks to this, there will be no more reason for VISITS, women will again start loving their children, and men, too. EVERYONE will go to dream under the trees. PEACE and PROSPERITY will return. JOY.

CHAPTER 9

I met Josias in May. It was early in the morning, and it was incredibly cold. After going out to smoke a cigarette, I went into the terminal restroom. There's nothing better than the automatic hand dryers to warm you up. You just have to take off your sweater and let the air flow over you. I closed my eyes and imagined an enormous engine propelling me with such force that I ultimately fly away. His rancid odour forced my eyes open. In the mirror, I saw him standing, not moving, with his black sweater full of holes.

'Can't you read? This is the women's room.'

He shrugged his shoulders just the way Vlad so often does. With the same despair.

'The dryers don't work in the men's room . . . I'm cold, too.'

A passenger, that's what I was. An anonymous traveller like all the ninety million others who, every year, arrive and pass through here. In a hurry, I needed to be in a hurry faced with his distress. Didn't I have a plane to catch? Fix my ponytail, turn around, leave. Find a flight, any flight. Head towards the right boarding gate. In other words, leave him. Leave him looking into the mirror, just as any other traveller would, because there can be no question of 'that'

when you're leaving. Maybe a few coins, except I don't have anything in my pockets. Really nothing. So, I turn around. But he's
blocking my way, me, the woman with green eyes, a rolling suitcase
found in front of a G7 taxi, me, the one who could be a mother, a
businesswoman, a tourist.

'I have a good place for the night, if you want, and you should
say yes, because they always manage to spot people like you.'

Had he found out from Liam, his half-mad brother who, when
he's in crisis, sometimes sees a person's entire past and future? Or
from Joséphine, their 'mother' who, though obese, finds the strength
to travel around the terminals, morning and night, observing everything, seeing everything, so that the eye of God, if He existed, could
do no better than she, or maybe by himself, one of those days after
fighting with his family when, to calm down, he has to walk around
the terminals seven times without stopping? Maybe it was that time
when, as he confided in me one day, he had come upon me late at
night observing the waltz of the runway sweepers, or the day I
arrived when, exhausted, I fell asleep on the ground in the hall of
the TGV Station. Josias smiles when I ask him the question, mutters
that he also likes mysteries. Probably my lack of movement during
my first days when I would remain seated for hours, shivering. It's
possible he noticed me then. Right before I understood.

Walk. Keep walking. Forty-eight hours sitting there were
enough for the information to get through to me. Walk, yes. Constantly. The only way not to be noticed by one of the one thousand
and seven hundred policemen assigned to security, or by one of the
seven hundred cameras that, 24/7, film the comings and goings of
everyone. Walk, go from one end of the terminals to the other,
retrace your steps. Go in a circle, because here all the connecting
terminals A-B-C-D-E-F form a huge 8. Blend into the crowds
while constantly moving to avoid the looks, those of the other

homeless, whose ranks I absolutely don't want to join, those of the police, of the staff, in short, of no fewer than one hundred thousand people.

Vlad, suddenly wary, looks at me straight in the eyes.

'One hundred thousand people, how do you know that?'

'I read it in their newspaper.'

'I thought you didn't read.'

'Before meeting you, no.'

'What else?'

'What, what else?'

'In their rag, what else, you didn't give me that one.'

'You didn't get it because it was dirty and torn. You told me you hated torn pages.'

'I hate them, you're right.'

'In September, the traffic at the Aéroports de Paris dropped by 10.4 per cent compared to the month of September 2013, with 7.2 million passengers going through, 4.9 million of whom at Paris-Charles-de-Gaulle. Aéroville attracted 7.2 million visitors, or close to 5 million fewer than the initial projection.'

'And you want me to believe there's something wrong with your memory?'

'There is, yes. That's why I try to retain everything I read.'

'My arse.'

He turns his back to me. I continue.

'All of the combined staff amount to 120,000 souls.'

'What's that to me?'

'I like knowing there are so many of them.'

Above all, I like the way they approach each other, the way they use the familiar *tu*. I don't know if it's because of their badges, but every time they meet, they say hello, always seeming to know each other.

'It's not like that elsewhere, is it?'

At the Quai de Seine counter, Lucien listens to me, his eyes wide.

'Elsewhere, you mean outside the airport? Man, it's as if you've never been out of here!'

I turn bright red. He bursts out laughing.

'Hey, I didn't mean to insult you! Here, I'll buy you another coffee for your pain. You have time, don't you? Your Paris–London doesn't leave until half past.'

I wonder how much he knows about me. The other day, when I confided in him my desire to change jobs, he leant into my ear, murmuring that, if I really tried, he was sure that I would find something . . .

'Because a woman like you can't stay like this.'

I acted like a girl who didn't understand, I even stupidly giggled, then some customers arrived and I seized the opportunity to slip away.

What does he really know? And from whom? Again, today, Lucien suggests that he knows a lot more than I might have thought.

We've known each other barely two months. I would pass in front of his cafe, and he would offer me a juice. Since then, it has become a ritual for us. He sometimes adds a sandwich, a plate of cookies, a yoghurt.

'I'd love to go to London with you, but with all the money I have to send my family, I have to count my pennies. Not to mention the Business Class ticket I want to give my mother. The day they finished building the school in my village, all the men, including my father, swore they'd never send their sons there. Furious, my mother walked to the government office—I'm talking 50 kilometres!—so they would force her idiotic husband to follow the law. How many times was she beaten because of that, and me, too! Everyone in the village regrets that now. Not long ago, everyone came to ask her forgiveness, begging her to get me to return from France so I could become head of the village instead of my brother.'

'And you don't want to?'

'It's because they think I'm rich. What's more, my brother . . . he is powerful. He holds really great powers. He is a wizard.'

'What do you mean, a wizard?'

He begins to laugh loudly.

'You white people, there's so much you don't know!'

All day long I walk, trying to do the usual things, reading newspapers, pulling my suitcase, comparing flights, talking to passengers without, however, managing to ease the panic that's rising up in me. What am I doing here? Can't they see that I'm lying to them?

Outside the windows that look on to the patio in T1, the spectacle of thousands of soap bubbles surging up into the sky, swept by red spotlights, soothes me. Kathy (badge), a waitress at Le Grand Comptoir cafe, confesses that she no longer notices the time go by since they created this decor. Before, she was a secretary. She landed this new job a month ago. She really likes it.

'The music of the different languages, above all.'

Flights for Istanbul, Madrid, Algiers, but the panic doesn't leave. I'm on a merry-go-round, I hold out my arm to catch the prize, but there's nothing, not the shadow of a prize, the merry-go-round turns for nothing. The first days, everything was new. Everything beckoned me. I slept well. I didn't have any headaches. Now I'm suffocating. I'm suffocating from pretending.

I go outside, and head towards the runways. When things are going badly, only the proximity of the aeroplanes calms me. Standing in front of the thundering of their engines, I scream, and it's like freeing the most intimate, the most inaccessible part of myself.

Yordan, a young Dutch spotter, approaches me.

'Did you hear about Pisa yesterday?'

'...'

'Right before take-off, on a Ryanair flight, a passenger had a panic attack and jumped off the plane.'

'What do you mean, jumped off?'

'I can show you the article if you want. And on an Egyptair flight, a python escaped from one of the passenger's bags. They had to make an emergency landing.'

I can't help laughing. You're never disappointed with these guys. Real crazies who spend their lives photographing all the planes in the world. An Air Canada appears from below the clouds. We look at it in silence, then a dozen others behind it. The evening slowly falls. He says goodbye and I remain standing opposite the runways, which are slowly lighting up, for over an hour, watching the planes arrive.

When, frozen by the cold, I push open the terminal door, the rumbling of their engines still echoes in me. How I love that din. It cleanses me.

BUNKER

Where checked luggage is deposited if, after several rounds of inspection, its contents are deemed suspicious.

CHAPTER 10

Sometimes I go from one terminal to another, something the other homeless don't do in the daytime. Most of them stay in T2, then, at night, sleep in T3, the low-cost airlines terminal. I never do that. Either I join Vlad in the underground corridors, or I choose a seat next to a well-dressed traveller, someone above suspicion, assuming the role of a wife, which sustains me for a night. On those nights, others join us: white-collar homeless who work in the city during the day; swarms of shadows who here and there grab a place on a chair, a bench. Some have bags, not many have suitcases. I sometimes count more than eighty. Shame on their faces. At dawn, they rush off to work, as if nothing was wrong.

Some nights I don't sleep. I really like the hours between midnight and 5 a.m., when travelling stops. No one moves any more. People, aeroplanes, all asleep. Only a few machines slide around, cleaning the vast floors. Cleaning men or women drive them, almost always in complete silence. They have three hours, not one minute more, to clean everything, otherwise there won't be enough time for the floors to dry and travellers risk slipping and falling. And so they concentrate, steering their machines a bit to the right, a bit to the left, scouring every inch so that everything glistens. Sometimes the moon shines in. The brightness of its rays reaches the still-damp floor and everything sparkles. I wander through the deserted halls, walk along the large windows. Not a single human being anywhere. I am the sole survivor of a cataclysm that has wiped them all out. In the cafes, the shadows of the chairs cast lines on the ground that tangle into infinity and which I enjoy following as if they granted me access to imaginary lands where all would be joyful. On the Arrivals level, I look through the windows at the empty baggage pick-up rooms. Everything is suspended. It's as if time is frozen. I take a cart, move ahead quickly and then jump on it. I'm gliding and laughing at the same time. Everything is so beautiful and so tranquil when no one is here. Farther away, on the tarmac, the enormous mass of aeroplanes shimmers, immobile. There is no one around them to anticipate the slightest movement; there is nothing left to wait for, nothing left to hope for. Under the clarity of the sky, the non-moving pavements are like abandoned roads. I set off majestically upon them.

I walk through my palace.

'Are you sure? You really don't want to have some coffee here?'

'Here' is the Emmaüs prefab building for homeless services, located at the end of T2B between the service roads. It was the morning after my second night. His name was Philippe, he'd been prowling around the airport for almost two years and was finishing up his very last rounds. I raised my head, and politely refused. I was really afraid he would force me to talk. But no. He was just trying to warn me that if I didn't want to be thrown out, I needed to learn a few things. Since then, I no longer walk around with plastic bags, a distinctive sign that you're homeless. And I never stop walking, or changing clothes (jackets, sweaters, scarfs, hats, glasses, which I find or steal), trying new hairstyles, opening doors, any doors, sometimes only to be yelled at, 'sorry, I'm lost, I'm looking for the lifts.' Coming and going, wandering outside, which the other homeless here avoid doing, unless they just go out for a smoke at the terminal entrances, but on the runway side or next to the airfreight zones, never. And yet, there is a lot to explore: 3,257 hectares, more than a third of the area of Paris, I learnt from an aeroplane captain. Except, when I beg Josias to follow me, he shakes his head, uncomfortable.

'There's nothing but roads over there, a real desert . . .'

He doesn't complete his sentence. Basically, I think the idea of finding himself alone facing the sky frightens him. Not me, I like it, that face-off, it soothes the void in me when the aeroplanes move around up there, it creates a vertigo, a bit like the day when the car danced. I remember now. Despite the shell that exploded, something protected me, a presence as sweet as that of the aeroplanes in the sky. When I see them approaching, their bodies slightly sloping down, noses pointed ahead, wheels opened to the air, I am reassured, consoled.

CHAPTER 11

Yesterday morning the airport was in turmoil. A bombing attempt at JFK had been thwarted just in time. Soldiers, trained dogs, security guards, plainclothes cops, they were all now on maximum alert. Qatching me get dressed, Vlad, worried, shakes his head.

'Wait a day or two before going up there.'

'Sorry, I have my Rio.'

On the Arrivals information board, flight AF4544 is 'flashing', which, in the language here, means it is going to land in less than ten minutes.

At the Espressamente cafe, two overly-excited Chinese people are arguing over a game of cards. Elena (badge), the waitress, waits nonchalantly for the storm to pass while polishing the 'Souvenirs de Paris' window.

In front of Arrivals, a group of 'saved' from the Church of the Last Judgement (with flags and caps) are singing psalms, holding hands.

In the background, a woman and her two children, a heartsick lover, an older couple, a handful of chauffeurs, and finally, leaning on the barrier, the man with the scarf whom I seemed to recognize the other day. This time, he is staring right at me and the memory returns. This is where I saw him before, over a month ago. Who waits for someone so long? My blood turns cold. A cop? I lower my eyes, immediately look up, remembering Vlad's lessons: 'Don't show them you're afraid, never raise your voice. Whatever happens, remain polite and respectful.'

On the news-channel screen:

Four members of the same family found in the family's apartment with their throats slit.

The stepfather is suspected.

Dig around in my purse. Take out the old mobile phone I stole two months ago. Tap a number, any number, speak in the voice of someone who is really travelling, a loud and clear voice. Play the role of someone who lives somewhere. Of someone who earns money, who has a job and, if the guy approaches me, admit that, since I've been unemployed, I've been hanging out here and have broken all ties with my family. But he doesn't move, just continues to observe me as if that truth, mine, were owed him. Just then the Rio passengers begin to emerge, disconnected—*all of them*—from the memory of those 228 people who, *all of them*, on the same flight, died during the night of 30 May between 23.10 and 23.14 above the Atlantic Ocean, miles and miles from any earth, the bodies of half of them never recovered.

I have fallen, too. An earth-shattering fall that didn't kill me, like them, but from which I emerged someone else. Before it happened, I lived my life. I no longer know which one, but a life that belonged to me *entirely* and which I must have worn out the way one wears out all that one thinks one possesses. Thus (this is the impression I keep of it), I must have talked about *my* body, *my* house, *my* relationships, *my* money, *my* profession, *my* husband, *my* legacy, *my* car, *my* family, *my* desires, *my* commitments, *my* hopes.

The light in the sky was grey. I got up, opened the armoire where, the day before, I had carefully placed my folded clothes. I unfolded them, and always put them on with that feeling of certainty that accompanies this type of life. There was a man (my husband?) who came home late in the evening. A man who kissed my neck. The car was blue and the house was as beautifully appointed as those in decorators' magazines. Not a speck of dust. Not an extra piece of furniture.

In the kitchen, a fridge filled with vegetables, because, in that life, healthy eating was considered essential. Life went on, unchanged, and I was that impeccable woman . . . No, that's impossible, I'm making this up. Opposite me, the man is still looking at me. I turn my head. I hurry away.

COPENHAGEN	AF1450	D61
PRAGUE	AF4900	D56
VALENCIA	UX1006	D70
LUXEMBOURG	LG8012	D75
MUNICH	AF1722	D63
MALENGA	UX1034	D57
VIENNA	OS412	D72

At the Quai de Seine counter, Lucien sees that I'm upset. He points to one of the empty chairs, but I prefer to stand, my back to all the cameras. He returns with a plate filled with gingerbread cookies.

'Eat. You'll feel better.'

He'd really like for me to tell him what's wrong, but how can I tell him what I'm experiencing, the shame, too, that of having fled that man whose mere look shattered the fortress I'm trying to build.

'Can you tell me? White or brown sugar?'

I shake my head, incapable of deciding.

'Anything else, my dear?'

No, nothing, Lucien. I'm just so afraid of that finger pointing at me, that shout: that's her! It would force me to turn around, to hear the shrieking in me.

'It's crazy, isn't it?'

'Sorry?'

Lucien sighs.

'This time, listen to me, right? He's just come into the shop, an Asian guy, forty–forty-five, going to Hong Kong, and he points at the vintage Château Pétrus 1985. Thierry tells him the price: 1,990 euros. The guy considers for no more than three seconds, then answers that it's fine. Thierry is asking if it's a gift, but the guy interrupts him—1,990 euros isn't enough, he still has a bit more. He then takes out a wad of bills and begins to count them. Then boom, he goes for a Château Yquem 1996! The guy pays, and then—this takes the cake!—just before leaving, he turns around and says, really happy: "It's for my sister, she loves good wine to make her vinaigrettes." Isn't that un-be-lievable?'

Lucien starts laughing. I mutter an excuse, then hurry off a second time.

Venice. Marseille. Lyon. Milan. Shanghai. Montréal. Cairo. Beirut. Toronto. Rome. Amsterdam. Casablanca. Geneva.

In the middle of the hall, children are on the ground. Farther away, their parents, exhausted, are sleeping on seats.

Terminal B. A Black man, bundled in his fur coat, looks frantically for his passport. Three Italian women in down coats watch him without taking off their sunglasses.

Terminal C. A tall blonde woman, business-class line: 'I'm late, so what? I have to leave, period.' Everything seems so absurd to me, so unreal. I push open the doors: the polar cold slaps my face.

'Madame, for 2G, here!'

I didn't see the driver of the shuttle open his door in front of me.

'*2G, here Madame! Here! Come!*'

I hesitate for a quarter of a second, '*Here Madame! Come!*' then I give in, probably to avoid the suspicious looks of the two Air Tunisia flight attendants who are probably wondering what I'm doing out in this cold watching cars when I could very easily do it from inside. Or maybe because the idea of leaving suddenly reassures me. I feel so vulnerable. In the shuttle, I'm the only traveller. Yassine (badge) asks me where I'm going (Hanover), if I've already travelled a lot (some). Does Bangkok have good night life? And Miami? Mauritius? I start laughing. I haven't been everywhere! He shrugs his shoulders. He hasn't been anywhere. But he definitely intends to go places one day. At the same time, it frightens him, those cities where they don't speak French. The shuttle goes by the Sheraton, gets back on the auto bridge, drives up above. Below, on the runways cleared by enormous ploughs, two Air France 737s are moving one behind the other towards the end of the tarmac while a very beautiful Japan Airlines 777 emerges from below the clouds. The shuttle moves. I try to respond as best I can to the torrent of questions Yassine continues to ask about Tokyo and its bars, Dubai at night, Hong Kong, Mumbai, New York.

On the left, the jetways of the superb Terminal S4, capable of welcoming as many as seven million travellers a year. I imagine the huge Place de Paris where, under its skylights, there are bars, restaurants, 'relaxation areas,' luxury shops . . .

I've arrived at the parking lot for 2G. In the distance, behind the embankments, the massive shape of a Saudi Arabian McDonnell Douglas reveals its bright blue wing decorated with a gold palm leaf. At the same time, a take-off, and in the sky, the vapour trail of a flight.

Inside the airport, no loudspeaker announcements. No crying children. Only the regular clacking of a rare rolling suitcase dragged over the white tile floor, and the sound of the wind that rushes in whenever anyone enters or leaves. A luggage-cart collector, pensive, is taking a coffee break among the waiting passengers. A bubble of calm that soothes me, but in which I unfortunately can't stay for more than two hours. 2G is too small to be invisible; sooner or later, I would end up being noticed. Looking at the tense people around me, I must indeed be the only one who is enjoying the tranquillity of the place. Whether they're leaving or arriving, they are all unsettled at the sight of the airport. 2G doesn't resemble anything. It is, moreover, only that. Nothing. And that's what I like. A collection of quickly constructed sheet metal which, with the slightest strong burst of wind, would fly away, the way I flew apart.

Vlad shakes his head.

'The past is the past. You can't go back.'

I don't say anything else, get back under the covers. This morning, when he saw that I wasn't going up to pay homage, he almost threw me out.

'So now what have you done?'

'Nothing, I just don't want to go up.'

'You don't want to go up, and you dare tell me that nothing has happened?'

'Don't get mad, Vlad.'

'I'll do what I want.'

'It's because of a guy. I have the feeling he knows about me.'

'Didn't I tell you not to go up, yes or no?'

'I don't even know if he's a cop.'

'Did he follow you?'

'No, but I'm still afraid.'

'Shit, I told you not to go up there!'

'. . .'

'Make me some coffee!'

I'm safe here. No one can find me, not even the guy I ran into in front of the doors from Rio. Who, on the surface, could imagine that people have chosen to live more than eight metres underground in subterranean corridors? Entrails that unfold over dozens and dozens of kilometres under the airport. Vlad told me one day that he had walked more than seven hours without seeing the end. He chose to settle down in the ducts of the electrical system. Just below are the conduits where the 'fluid' passes, where all the liquids flow, but no one lives there.

'They might piss in there, or they might take a shit.'

'Who's "they?"'

Vlad doesn't know. Since he's been here, he has never run into other 'inhabitants,' even though he's heard there were three others.

'Who told you that?'

'I read, I'm informed.'

'But where are they, if they live here?'

'How should I know? Anyway, leave me alone, I don't need any-one, much less a woman who never stops asking questions!'

I don't answer, just look around at the long, wide pipes that go along the ceiling and walls. Some are so hot you can't touch them. We dry our clothes on those. Others, thinner, emit strange noises, like nails on a chalkboard or like pots that clang at the bottom of a well. The corridor is at most three metres wide, but you can easily stand up in it, and that's pretty good. The light, an infinite series of hanging electric bulbs, never goes out. Vlad has thrown a mattress and some covers on the ground, arranging kitchen utensils, magazines, newspapers, books, and even a transistor radio around it. Vlad loves listening to music and, here, he can even turn the volume way up without disturbing anyone. I don't know why he trusts me, or why he adopted me. I sometimes tell myself that it's so he no longer has to 'fuck with the human race', as he puts it. However, I do sense another reason. Something connected to what I was. But who? A woman whose life, after a marriage and an accident, has come undone? A crazy woman escaped from an asylum? Or maybe the other one who really frightens me and whom I reject with all my being?

 CHAPTER 12

'"*I want a hot chocolate*"—Repeat!'

'*I want a hot chocolate.*'

'Very good. Now: *I want some cold milk.*'

'*I want some cold milk.*'

'And now: je ne veux pas d'eau.'

'*I do not want water . . .*'

'*Any water!*'

'Sorry—*any water.*'

'If you want to get by, you can't make any mistakes.'

'At least tell me why you're so keen on teaching me everything you know.'

'What I know never helped me at all, but maybe it will be of some use to you.'

'I don't understand.'

'That's what saves you.'

He walks away, wearily turns on his transistor radio, begins to turn round and round, standing as straight as an arrow, moving to deafening electronic music. I'm suddenly embarrassed. Embarrassed at seeing how much pain he truly is in, and which I can do nothing about, not even offer a gesture of tenderness, the gentlest kiss here would only open the wound. So I don't move and keep watching him until he exhausts himself as he continues to spin faster and faster, as if he is trying to reach the pinnacle of a trance when the body, losing all control, collapses on the ground with a dull sound while the music, that of the world, keeps going, more frenzied than ever.

I don't know what country Vlad comes from. A country in the East, but which one? Hungary? Romania? Estonia? Kosovo? And I don't know why he came to France, or how long he's been here. A long time ago, 'in another life', as he says, he was an English teacher.

'But I'll never teach again.'

'Maybe the guys from Emmaüs could help you with the paperwork.'

'No, no one.'

'Why no one, Vlad?'

'No one, that's all.'

I met Josias right before him. Vlad was two weeks later. I was trying to open the metal doors of the mechanical area on the first sub-level of T2C which open onto the service roads. I was looking for a place to lie down. I was more than tired of sleeping on seats, and sleeping on the ground in T3 with all the others was out of the question, even if Josias swore on all the gods that no one would bother me.

'If I talk to them, the Russians will protect you, believe me. With all the favours I do for them. . .'

No, it would have been better to sleep standing up. Except, that evening, my feet were terribly swollen. At this rate, soon I wouldn't even be able to put on my shoes. I had to find a place where I could lie down in peace. I started by exploring the hallways located under T2B, but found only locked doors. Then, on the first sub-level of T2C, the length of the service roads, I fell upon a series of doors that I had never noticed. One after the other, I tried without success to open them, until I felt a hand on my shoulder. The man standing in front of me, well-built, white skin, blue eyes, was him, Vlad. We stood for a few moments looking at each other. I tried to come up with the simplest thing to say while I attempted to figure out what sort of man I was dealing with. As for him, I don't know, but it was as if in seeing my face he had been surprised, the expression in his eyes going from violence to astonishment.

'What are you doing here?'

'I'm . . . I'm lost.'

'Are you looking for someone?'

'I'm looking for a place to sleep.'

'Are you kidding me?'

I then tried to get away, but he blocked my way with his arm. He didn't have a badge or a uniform. What did he want?

'It's OK. Follow me.'

I watched him without moving.

'Do you want to sleep somewhere, yes or no?'

'I didn't say with someone.'

'Who said I was going to sleep with you?'

'That's not it.'

'Then what, if I tell you I'm not going to hurt you?'

He lowered his head, and repeated in a broken voice.

'I swear to you, no harm.'

He took my hand.

'Come on!'

The underworld. A maze of hallways. Oppressive darkness.

'Watch out for the pipes, they're very hot!'

'You sleep here?'

'Not far, be quiet.'

We walked for ten minutes, and then, in a corner, his mattress on the ground covered with books and newspapers, a pile of scattered clothes, some hanging off the ducts, a little gas stove, a transistor radio. I almost laughed. He guessed that laugh in me, I'm sure, it pleased him. I lay down, waiting for him to undress. Very quickly, and rather abruptly, he came. I didn't feel a thing. Not pain, not pleasure. I did everything so that he wouldn't notice.

Since then, he sometimes asks me, and I always say yes. And he introduces me to books, he teaches me English, a bit of Russian, too, he opens his 'lair' to me whenever I appear.

CLEANER

A vehicle created at Roissy-Charles-de-Gaulle to clean its 20,000 runway lights. It uses crushed nutshells, which are both soft and sufficiently abrasive, to clean every millimetre of the lights using a camera placed at the end of the arm located at the front of the vehicle. Ten years ago, the cleaning was done by hand using detergent, then with a power washer and hot water.

 CHAPTER 13

This morning, I got up very early to have time to buy as many provisions as I could at the Petit Casino store in T2B. Lucien doesn't work at that hour, and Josias is sleeping with his group. As for the man with the scarf, I have to count on luck not to run into him (sunglasses, scarf around my hair, orange suitcase this time, a long, dark-purple coat).

The day before, Vlad handed me some bills that he took out of a metal box.

'Buy what you want, but buy enough so you won't have to go back up for a while, OK?'

We can get water from the tap on the service road. At night, there's never anyone there. But we need everything else: bread, jam, canned meat, cereal, concentrated milk, coffee, sugar, chips, cheese, candy, fruit.

In the store, my mountain of purchases elicits a suspicious look from Claire (badge), the clerk.

'There are ten in our group, and we missed our connection yesterday, so we slept at the airport, and we're starving!'

She started to laugh, reassured.

'Where are you headed?'

'Caracas, Venezuela.'

She hands me some recyclable bags, advises me to double them.

'After spending all that, you don't want your breakfast to end up on the ground, right?'

I thank her, and hear her say in a warm voice, 'Have a good trip!' I walk quickly to the restrooms opposite the Disneyland Resort buses, and wash my face. What I wouldn't give for a shower at the Ibis Hotel! But with all these bags, I'm highly suspicious, and Vlad is waiting for me.

The sun hasn't come up yet; I'm only a shadow for the cameras. I find a cart, put my bags in it, take off my sunglasses, my scarf, undo my hair, and go back down to sub-level 1. Sitting in front of their screens, seeing the new look I have, with a cart no less, they can only assume I'm one of the forty-two homeless people that Emmaüs takes care of here. The association's centre isn't far, and it isn't unusual to see a few 'figures' wandering around the area.

Outside, I open the metal door and make sure no one is around, then take the bags, one by one, down the ladder on the wall, regrouping at the bottom. It takes ten minutes to get to Vlad's camp. It's not very far. But each time I go through the corridor towards it, I'm seized with panic, as if this subterranean place is going to close up on me for ever.

'I said Lavazza!'

'What's the matter? You're shivering.'

'It's nothing.'

'But Vlad . . .'

'Don't look at me like that, I've just caught a cold, that's all. Do you have any change?'

'Yes, here.'

'Coffee with milk for me.'

'Do you want sugar?'

'Ugh . . . sugar in coffee!'

We drink in silence, I'm sitting on the mattress, he's buried under the covers. I can tell he has a fever; he's sweating profusely. I approach him, put a damp cloth on his burning forehead. He lets me do it, then goes back to sleep. I look at the walls, taking in the idea of staying enclosed here. The hours go by. Vlad's eyes are still shut. I scarcely eat, keep staring at the walls that are dripping with humidity, worrying about his cough, which is getting worse. I finally wake him up.

'No, I don't need any medicine! And don't think about going to get any! Anyway, they're just a bunch of shit, all those pills!'

Maybe he's afraid that I'm going to abandon him, or that I'll be caught. Then he would be alone, for ever. Between two prolonged naps, I ask him if I can listen to some music, but he says no, under the pretext that I might break 'his' machine. He's just too ill to listen to anything, and I don't argue.

Up above, I hear only the dampened noise of the aeroplanes on the runways, a roiling that rumbles above my head.

I suddenly start laughing. What if I really were a homeless person? What if the rare memories that surface (that accident, those two little girls, that marriage, that icy woman) were the product of a mind that had always been deranged? How many times have I replayed the scene of the woman or man who, seeing me, would call me by my name? He or she would approach, tell me my story, and I would stand there frozen. Nothing that he or she tells me would mean anything to me. To the point of exasperating them. *It's impossible! You're doing this on purpose!* Then blackness, always more oppressive, darker.

'You know, even if I die I don't give a shit.'

'No, Vlad, no one doesn't give a shit about dying.'

'I don't.'

I wipe his forehead, try to get him to drink. When he finally goes back to sleep, the memories that recently returned rush back. I try to close my eyes to escape them, but they keep spinning in my head. I finally fall asleep, too.

Dream. The Arrival doors open, like a burst of wind, onto a cloud of men and women. There are so many of them that when they go by, under their feet, the borders give way and disappear. On earth, in the blink of an eye, as far as the horizon, their mass forms a single and sole land.

'You have friends, don't you? You didn't plan to spend your whole life here, did you?'

'Vlad, did you say something?'

'Stand up inside!'

'Vlad, I'm afraid, I beg you, answer me, I hear voices . . . '

'Your father and mother are dead, don't you remember?'

'Dead!!! Vlad, wake up!!!'

'No, you're crazy to shout like that!'

'My memory, Vlad, memories, I . . . I don't want to, I'm afraid.'

'If you don't want to remember, then read! And now leave me alone!'

CHAPTER 14

Read—he's right. How many times has the simple description of a landscape soothed me? Except that since those words have resurged, my brain is churning. Are my parents really dead? And that man beside me, those two little girls, that car accident? Is it because they're all dead, too, that no one has tried to find me? That big house, why haven't I been sent back to it? Wasn't that where I lived?

I think again about what Josias told me about his life when he lived on the streets. Not a day went by that he wasn't beaten up by cops or thieves or other homeless. Not to mention the cold and hunger that gripped his stomach all the time. Like all the ones who end up here, he thought the same thing: paradise! Free heating 24/7, toilets readily available, comfortable seats, not to mention the Emmaüs guys who, every morning at nine o'clock, serve hot coffee to anyone who feels like going to their prefab office.

There, you can 'talk' while eating cookies. You can learn to read, cook and fill out the administrative paperwork which sometimes gets you benefits, and even work.

There are free rubbers in bins next to the coffee machine. The youngest visitors are the first to help themselves. Most of them are prostitutes. Sometimes, there's a delivery of old airport-personnel clothing: there's something for every taste, every size. When a conflict arises, you can talk about it there and, most often, things end well. No one wants to be kicked out of here. The airport personnel are so nice, many even try to help. How many times have Josias and his mother received a bit of food from a cleaning woman? If travellers are sometimes surprised to encounter 'figures,' they cross their paths without commenting. They're not going to miss their plane because of some homeless person. It's only when one of the 'figures' has a fit or starts banging his head on the windows like a crazy person, screaming for everyone to get out, as Robocop did, that you hear some murmurings of discontent, but not very much compared to what happens outside.

'In Paris, some thugs broke Liam's arm for two lousy euros, and Jene, the Puerto Rican guy they ended up deporting, some guys sliced up his stomach with a box-cutter real good! Things like that would never happen here.'

I nod my head. The airport protects us. It is our cocoon and, for me, my only true memory. Vlad, in a wheezing voice, asks for some water. I hand him a glass, wipe his burning forehead with a damp cloth. Up there, in the distance, a plane hits the ground. How many of them are inside here? A hundred? Two hundred? What were they doing before, 'out there'? Did they get divorced? Take exams? Seen childhood friends again? Vlad keeps groaning, I walk in circles like a caged lion. All those things I might hear from their mouths. Sometimes, it only takes a minute, I catch the name of a city, a street, I walk there, I get denser. But here, in the silence? I raise my head, hesitate for a moment, wanting to rejoin them. No, the guy recognized me, I need to let some time go by. I sit on the mattress and open my suitcase. Looking at my things, I come upon Liam's notebook. The last time, it took me several hours to decipher his tiny writing. But, I don't have anything else to do, and there's that badge-holder to earn. Unless Josias was tricking me. He has been known to lie. To shout. To fight, too. Bare-fisted and bloody. Like all the others here.

LIAM'S NOTEBOOK, 2

(edited)

If they think that He hasn't seen everything, they're wrong. The girl shouted and all the others who weren't wearing Letters, that's why they were taken BY FORCE supposedly to be returned to their countries but He knows that they're lying, the Dalai Lama intervened, except he wasn't wearing any Letters either, he just barely got away!

Everyone understood it was the end. He saw all that, the girl who clawed at the ground with her fingernails until they bled, the tears of HUGO BOSS but he couldn't intervene or maybe he had been caught too and thrown into aeroplanes that supposedly took people to their countries when they were being sent to THE TEN DESTINATIONS FOR 1,000 EUROS!

Even though the women to save their children preferred to freeze their babies rather than have Them go through that! But it didn't help because they still found the babies and now the women are judged, and as a consequence fear is growing everywhere!

Everywhere they make it known that they are sending tonnes of food 'over there' because people 'over there' need vitamins and a pile of powdered food, but if they say that, it's so everybody feels obliged to contribute and everyone does contribute! He knows that it is another of their manipulations and that that money is used only to send more and more people to THE TEN DESTINA-TIONS, and we must stop that! But to succeed, we must stop trips and information in order to assemble as quickly as possible all the Letters into one place. All of them, otherwise, up to the last of the last of them, they will end up being sent to THE TEN DESTINATIONS, which will cause THE END OF HUMANKIND. He knows what He's talking about, they wrote to him, anyway (they don't even try to hide it any more!): two of them poisoned their parents to be able to use their inheritance for A LOVELY TRIP! The time is thus serious because soon the same ones will do everything in their power so that EVERYONE TRAVELS EVEN MORE so that ALL, due to the TOURIST OFFERS, will agree to be CONVEYED where they shouldn't and without even being beaten any more! And if this happens then THE BIG SECRET that He alone knows will no longer serve ANYTHING and we will probably witness something so horrible that it will not even any longer be a question of climate disruption or the extinction of species . . .

That's why He has decided to act among the Letters so that they can be assembled as quickly as possible! And He isn't worried that ALL OF THEM appear surprised and act as if they didn't understand! It is a ruse on their part to trick the Censor and avoid being stricken! NAF NAF, moreover, is already muttering something in the ear of MY DIAMS which itself is advising NIKE . . .

Soon, thanks to HIM, THEY WILL ALL give each other the DATE OF THE GREAT ASSEMBLING and it will be THE END OF THE REIGN OF THE CENSOR, which, in this great chaos and in spite of the suffering of frozen babies, of the girl brought by FORCE, the tears of HUGO BOSS, and the saddened face of the Dalai Lama, delights him.

CHAPTER 15

The days go by, all gloomy. I read without reading, sleep as much as possible, cling to Vlad when he awakens. One evening, his fever raging, he grabs my hand, speaks in semi-delirium of 'his war', then of his wife and children, all three assassinated. When he awakes, I try to question him, but he's evasive. He never had a wife, much less children. I push a bit, but he begins to cough so violently that I stop.

'Vlad, let me at least go get some medicine.'

'What about the guy who recognized you? What do you think will happen if he catches you? And what medicine? I've just caught a nasty cold that takes time to get better.'

Every hour that goes by is torture. I stay lying down, immobile, without the will to get up. Everything is so sad here: the filth, the damp walls. Up there, in the airport terminals, the threat of being unmasked at any moment forced me to stay on guard. I was a hunted animal, but here? I curl up in a ball under the covers. Sleep, that's all I have left. Sleep, slide, hold my hand out to the void.

'Let's play hide and seek!' shouts a little boy.

The little girl begs her big sister with her eyes, and she finally gives in with a sigh.

'I'll count to thirty!' the little boy says.

Shouts and laughter everywhere. All the children start running.

'One . . . Two . . .'

The two little girls run down a grassy hill.

'Over there, a bush!' whispers the older one, 'go ahead, hide, I'll find another place, there's not enough room for us both.'

But the little girl shakes her head. She doesn't want to leave her sister. Annoyed, the bigger one scans the yard with her eyes. 'Twenty!' shouts the seeker behind them.

'I know, there, against the stone wall, the trunk of the old apple tree!'

Running, she pulls her little sister along. But, not there either, there's not enough room for both of them. In the bushes she notices a passageway between the stones. What luck! Her head lowered, she squeezes through first, making sure that her little sister doesn't hurt herself in the thorn bushes. Hurrah, they've gone through the wall! No one will ever find them on this side, that's certain. She raises her head to look at the sky. The sun is still high. The heat is crushing. She spits in her hands, wipes the scrapes on her knees with the back of her hand without paying attention to her little sister who has let go of her hand.

'Come here!' she hears. 'Come on, I've found something!'

She turns around and freezes . . .

I awaken, drenched in sweat. What the little girl found is something horrible. But what exactly? Everything in my head is a jumble. Why wasn't the big girl's face the same as before? But she was wearing the same dress and the same hairstyle! Are there three sisters, then? If so, why haven't I ever seen them together, and what's the connection between this well story and the accident? Next to me, Vlad is coughing. A thousand questions spin around in my head, but there are no answers.

I can't stand it any more. I decide to go fill up some water bottles on the surface.

A gust of frigid air. Snow.

Stunned, I contemplate the world that has become completely white. Suddenly everything is perfectly beautiful and calm. Don't move any more, die here. The snowflakes fall so delicately on my body. Soon, I'm covered with them, and it's like entering fully into absence.

★

From behind, she is sitting, her knees folded, beyond any contact with the world. How old is she and how has she been able to get into this space entirely enclosed by glass? If people call for her, she can't hear them, and if some try to approach her, they bump against the transparent wall that separates her from the world. She is sitting, staring into space; sitting in a silence in which she has been motionless since the night of time. One would really like to know the colour of her eyes, know if she's cold. At times, someone bumps against the window, but it is as if she has decided to close herself off from all sound. She is sitting, her chin resting on her knees, which she has folded as if to keep herself warm. No one can say when nor how she arrived. In this place where she is staying, seasons don't exist, only the wind shudders. And yet, it is as if she doesn't feel it. In fact, one might say that she doesn't exist. But her heart beats, and some nights you can hear it.

Did she decide to settle here, or was she caught in a trap? That, too, would be good to know. It's so painful to see her like that, her arms hugging her knees, on the verge of tears. Sometimes, she rocks back and forth, but without ever turning around, as if she no longer wants to see those who are watching her. Does she sleep? Does she dream? No one can say because no one can approach her. From time to time, people try to break the window using a bat or a hammer. Concerned, others form a circle around them, wondering if it's OK to do that. And then, nothing, the glass doesn't break.

Heads lowered, everyone goes back to their side, without having seen her budge. The days after such days, a great fatigue settles in and everyone tries to forget her: one, while cleaning his house; another, by buying some Nutella; another, by driving at 180 kmph on the highway; another, by bursting into tears; another, by railing against the stupidity of TV programmes; another, by catching a cold; the last one, by tossing his last coins at a guy in the subway. The days go by, they ultimately return.

Some say that she is their wounded part. Others go even further. She is the cries of raped women, those of martyred children, hated, butchered peoples. Without her, the shrieking of victims on TV would become so audible that it would burst their eardrums. One listens to those, stunned.

No one really knows why she is there nor why they would really like, one day, to hear her speak, if only a word. There is such a sadness here. A single word, and the glass—some assert this—would shatter. But what is that word? And who would whisper it to her?

It is snowing now. It is snowing on her skin and on the world. She leans her head back a bit, opens her mouth, swallows a snowflake. Is it a miracle? And yet she doesn't turn around. She feels so good under this coat of snow, so good letting herself be buried, forgetting all the pain.

Then dawn appears with the crowd and the explosion of its take-offs.

And it is as if, from her eyes, a veil has been torn.

 CHAPTER 16

When I go back into the terminal, I come across a small announcement, which I read three times:

WARNING! EBOLA VIRUS!

**IF WITHIN 7 DAYS FOLLOWING YOUR ARRIVAL IN FRANCE
YOU HAVE A FEVER ABOVE 38°C (OR ACHES AND FATIGUE)
COUGHING AND TROUBLE BREATHING,
IMMEDIATELY CALL 15 OR YOUR OWN DOCTOR.**

How did I not make the connection with Vlad's illness? I run back, and kneel next to him.

'Vlad, you must see a doctor.' He doesn't wake up. I shake him.

'Vlad, it's possible some passenger has passed this nasty virus on to you!'

His eyes partially open, and he mutters a few words in a language I don't understand.

'Vlad, can you hear me?'

He slowly nods his head.

'In my pocket, look ... '

His finger remains suspended. I shake him, but he doesn't move. Go get help? But who? I have never spoken about Vlad to Josias. Lucien? He doesn't work at night, and what would he say? Then who? I'm not strong enough to carry him alone. The guys from Emmaüs? The police?

'Where did you find him? What country is he from? Do you have his papers? How did he get here? How did you know he was there? Since when? *Who are you?*'

My mind churns and I can't fall asleep, I wipe his forehead, begging him to get better, then, remembering his gesture, start digging in his trouser pockets, find the yellowed photo of a man surrounded by a woman and two children: a little girl and a boy, around eleven and five years old. It takes me a few seconds to see that it's he, Vlad. He's radiant, surrounded by his family, sitting against the wall of his house in the country that was his. Shaken, I linger on his face, then on those, so peaceful, of his wife and two children. In what country were they killed? Which war? I start going through his things, and at the bottom of a suitcase I find an old student-ID card with a black-and-white photo in which Vlad is again showing his superb smile. The word 'Yugoslavia' finally reveals his country of origin. In the pocket of another pair of trousers, I find a poem typed on a sheet of paper, in the margin of which someone had written '*I wish I had understood.*'

> *I wandered lonely as a cloud*
> *That floats on high o'er vales and hills*
> *When all at once I saw a crowd,*
> *A host, of golden daffodils;*
> *Beside the lake, beneath the trees,*
> *Fluttering and dancing in the breeze.*

Continuous as the stars that shine
And twinkle on the milky way,
They stretched in never-ending line
Along the margin of a bay:
Ten thousand saw I at a glance,
Tossing their heads in sprightly dance.

The waves beside them danced; but they
Out-did the sparkling waves in glee:
A poet could not but be gay,
In such a jocund company:
I gazed—and gazed—but little thought
What wealth the show to me had brought:

For oft, when on my couch I lie
In vacant or in pensive mood,
They flash upon that inward eye
Which is the bliss of solitude;
And then my heart with pleasure fills,
And dances with the daffodils.

—William Wordsworth

A night in hell, monitoring his every breath. I beg him to fight the illness with all his strength, to think of the day when he'll be well, when he can tell me the names of his family, the reason why he kept that poem. But he doesn't hear me, fights to fill his lungs with a bit of air, coughs the way someone would spit.

'Vlad, this can't continue, I'm going to get help.'

He doesn't answer, doesn't move.

'Vlad?'

He emits a weak gurgle, coughs again, exhausted.

'I'll be back, Vlad, do you hear me? I'll be right back.'

CHAPTER 17

Upstairs, it's still dark outside. On the other side of the metal door, snow has covered the world. On the runway side, six staggered Boschung snow removers, followed by two de-icers and two 'snow blower' trucks, are working tirelessly on the southern roads, throwing off gigantic clouds of white power that, in the headlights, rise up, and burst into glitter. The airport is still deserted. I move along, trying not to walk too quickly. At this hour, the planes aren't flying, what reason would I have to be in a hurry?

Going through the terminals, the pleasure of being back here is so strong that for a short moment it chases away my fear of watching Vlad die. Everything is still in its place: display screens, counters, benches, sleeping passengers, floor, escalators, rolling walkways. Everything, as if the airport had been waiting for me.

**WITH THE 'FLYING BLUE' CARD,
LET YOURSELF BE TRANSPORTED . . .**

A beep from the lift. Three cameras are pointed at me. Assume the correct demeanour. Read the information. Pretend to be a passenger who, after a few hours' dozing is going to her car in the parking lot. The doors open. Descent.

Now what?

Mainly, don't think. I'm here for Vlad. For him alone. In the back of the parking lot, behind their eleven carts, all three of them are snoring. I move one of the carts to get to where Josias is sleeping, and grab an empty can just before it falls.

'Josias? Josias, can you hear me? Josias?'

All three of them sit up in unison. A dishevelled Joséphine looks at me.

'What the hell! You can't just wake people up like that!'

I decide to ignore her.

'Josias, I need your help. We have to go quickly.'

Dumbfounded, Joséphine turns to her son.

'You . . . know her?!'

Josias stares at me, wondering where I came from and if I hadn't turned completely mad. Joséphine shakes him by the shoulders.

'I asked you a question!'

But Josias doesn't have time to respond. Liam, eyes bulging, begins to shout:

'I told you they'd come to get us!'

Then Josias leaps forward, and I barely avoid the first blow his brother was aiming at me.

'Fuck, Liam, it's the girl from National Education, the one who's editing your journals!'

For Joséphine, that's the last straw.

'What the hell is going on? Who is this girl?'

Frozen, Josias and Liam bow their heads.

'Ah, it looks like I have two real shitheads!'

Hang in there, think of Vlad, of Vlad's cough, summon that cold, authoritarian voice, so foreign and yet so familiar, which I used to use with *those people*, because *I didn't like them*, I really couldn't stand them.

'Josias has to follow me now. I need his help.'

'Do you hear, Jackass, the lady needs you!'

'But, Mom . . .'

'Shut up!'

I take a step forward, look Joséphine in the eyes.

'Someone is dying. Josias has to help me.'

Joséphine seems to be thinking. Strangely, it is Liam who, in a suddenly calm voice, says:

'She's right, Mom. The future of the world depends on it. Say yes.'

In the lift, Josias explodes.

'What you've done is serious! Serious, do you hear!'

I shrug my shoulders, indifferent. By now, Vlad is perhaps already dead.

'Hurry up!'

He follows me, amazed, through the terminals, freezes when he sees me open the metal door that opens onto the underground passageways.

'We're not going down there, are we?'

'Yes, we are.'

'Shit, you know people who . . .'

'His name is Vlad, don't ask me where he comes from, or what he's doing here and how I know him. He's really sick. I can't carry him.'

'Vlad?!'

'Vlad.'

'You've had a guy all this time and you never told me!'

'Josias, help me bring him up, and afterwards I'll explain everything, OK?'

'I looked for you everywhere!'

'I'm sorry.'

'*Sorry*?!'

'Josias, please.'

'And why should I do this?'

'. . .'

'You've slept with him?'

'. . .'

'Fuck, you've slept with him.'

I don't look at him, we go down the rungs of the ladder one by one. Under the weak glow of the electric bulbs, I move faster and faster. Too bad if he doesn't want to follow me, I have to get back to Vlad no matter what. Behind me, in the distance, I hear Josias grumbling, furious, appalled. I no longer pay attention to him, keep going, almost running. Footsteps behind me! I turn around, my heart beating. Cops or guards hate squatters from down here. When they're forced to 'descend', they ask to be accompanied by the Emmaüs guys. Fear blends with a feeling of outrage. They haven't chosen this profession to track down the remains of men in the depths of the airport. Some seek vengeance by destroying the first squatter site they find, siccing their dogs on the people sleeping there. I mustn't fall upon one of them, or else, as they are fond of saying on such occasions: 'You're screwed.'

No, it's Josias, furious. I don't care. I'm so happy he followed me. When he sees Vlad, his anger suddenly dissipates: a pasty body buried in the covers. He's barely breathing, and his gaze is so distant that it looks like he's already dead. I kneel next to him. He answers with a wheeze followed by extreme trembling, then collapses again. Josias reacts faster than I do.

'Get him on my back, hurry up!'

All of a sudden, his voice has changed. Death in front of his eyes, no way. And too bad if the guy weighs a ton, he's suddenly ready to do anything to save him. Seeing such life force, I begin to cry. And the tears continue as Josias runs in front of me, Vlad on his back.

'Meet me in T2F at Carlion's. That's where they'll take him when they stop me.'

'Josias, I . . . '

'Oh, no, no bowing and scraping, please! You've fucked things up enough with all this!'

CHAPTER 18

There aren't any vacant seats in front of the double doors of the EMS opposite Exit 17. Outside, taxis emerge from their holding area one after the other. Some have waited underground more than three hours in what some of them call their 'Guantanamo' before finally being able to get a customer. And there's no way to turn around, scarcely the opportunity to use the toilet! Which explains their increasingly frequent run-ins with chauffeur-driven cars and ride hustlers.

In the distance, I notice Georges, a black T-shirt, prayer beads around his neck, who is approaching while pushing his cart. He stops in front of the EMS doors, shouting that everyone should fuck themselves, which makes him laugh loudly. The door opens, Carlion appears.

'Can you stop shouting, Georges? What's that T-shirt? You're going to catch cold!'

'It's not my fault, Doctor, they stole everything from me!'

'Right, it's always the same. What exactly are you here for? To eat the cookies?'

'Cookies? I don't have any teeth! I need my pills!'

'What about your Vitale card?'

'I did what I was supposed to, Doctor, it's good, it's renewed!'

'Great!'

'The others steal, no one says anything. But I do what I'm supposed to, and I get yelled at. There's no justice.'

'There never has been.'

Georges starts dancing.

'Georges, how do you want your medication, in gel capsules?'

'Yeah, and not 10 milligrams—5. See, I still have a memory!'

'You're joking!'

'No way! You know, there's someone up there who's jealous because I'm tight with the managers at Chez Maxim's. So? People are allowed to respect me, aren't they?'

Carlion goes back through the double doors, Georges follows behind him, spinning around a few times. I really want to follow them, to ask how Vlad is doing. But Carlion would stare at me, bewildered. If there's someone who knows all the homeless at the airport, it's he; although he would hesitate to use the word 'homeless'. Social ghosts, at best, or disturbed migrators. There are forty-two at Roissy, and he knows all of them, because you have to see a doctor to get your meds refilled. Imagine his reaction at learning I'm one of the gang! Carlion doesn't like to miss anything, and really hates it when someone pulls something over on him. So I change my mind, wait for Georges who, smiling broadly, comes out without seeing me, still dancing. Go ask him? No.

I'm not of their world.

A young guy goes in holding his arm. Just as the doors are closing, I hear a voice asking where the instant coffee is, then silence. Could they have had Vlad transferred to the Robert-Bélanger Hospital in

Aulnay? That's where they transfer serious cases, primarily the dead—twenty-three a year, per Josias, who got the number from Carlion: illnesses, accidents, strokes, heart attacks. No, if Vlad were dead, Josias would be here to let me know.

A young African man appears, staring at the ground, surrounded by two plainclothes cops. He'll soon be deported, he knows. Just then, a group of adolescents, wild with joy, leaving to study Spanish in Spain, passes by. He begs me with his eyes. I sense he's ready for anything. But I lower my eyes, imagining the fate that would await me if the same cops descended on me. Their hands on my body. Their hatred. When I raise my head, he's no longer there, and I wonder where they took him. 'Over there,' Josias would mutter, then change the subject. Over there where, every year, several of them decide to open their veins.

The EMS doors open again, and this time it's Vlad. He's on a stretcher, an oxygen mask on his face. I get up, trembling. Is he going to die? Distraught, I see the stretcher disappear into the ambulance that takes off, siren blaring. A guard catches my eye. I don't have a suitcase, not even a purse. I turn away, my arms wrapped around me. A few metres away, a little boy accompanied by a flight attendant raises his large eyes to me. The attendant accompanying him is carrying his teddy bear. His hand is bleeding. Soon they both disappear. I start shivering. It's time to return to the camp if I don't want to be noticed.

On Level -1, I barely avoid two workers. I open the metal door, and am careful when I close it so it doesn't make any noise. I then go down the ladder rung by rung. I proceed cautiously, the rancid smell makes me gag.

When I get to the camp, I hold back a sob when I see the empty bed, then I freeze at the sound of steps. Someone is coming. I scarcely have time to pull on my coat and grab my purse when a voice behind me shouts:

'Hey, you, over there!!!'

Without thinking, I start running towards a no man's land where I've never ventured before. Behind me are at least four of them. Some are shouting in a foreign language. Russian? I dash through the passages, to the right, to the left, without knowing where I'm going. They give up. Too many turns and corridors here. In the distance I hear their shouts echoing, their kicking against the pipes. Cops would have turned back before now. Who are they? Gang members sent by Josias, furious at my relationship with Vlad? Needy fugitives? I cower down to warm up, breathe in and out as quietly as possible. After what seems like an eternity, I finally find the courage to stand up. It's the smell of something burning that leads me back. I make a final left turn and discover the destruction: Vlad's books burned with lit gas. The mattress ripped up. The transistor crushed underfoot. The clothing torn. My suitcase forced open and the contents gone. I walk by the camp without turning around, climb the ladder, open the door and, my mind empty, I run.

DUPE

A passenger who has checked-in twice.

 CHAPTER 19

Over the loudspeakers, the warm voice of a young woman asks Mr and Mrs Toural to please go to the information booth at T2C where their son Cédric is waiting for them.

There are people everywhere. Due to the bad weather, the boards are posting flight delays of one to two hours. Everyone is stomping around and complaining. Exhausted and discouraged, I sit down on a bench and count the little bit of money I have left. A guard is sizing me up. Wanting to avoid him, I stand up and start walking away towards T2B when a hand grabs me from behind, forcing me to turn around. It's Liam, his eyes bulging; he's trembling all over. In the blink of an eye he is stuffing something into my purse.

'For you . . .'

Without giving me time to react, he again plunges his hand into his pocket and takes out a notebook.

'Could you please edit this one, too? Could you?'

He grabs my arm, and squeezes it tightly.

'You alone hold the world, you alone!'

I nod OK, wooden. He releases his grip, and runs off. A man walks up, smiling.

'Brigitte Garaudis?'

My heart leaps. The man is staring at my face.

'You're not one of the Elsesia group?' I laugh nervously.

'No, sorry.'

The guy walks away. I close my eyes to get a hold of myself. For a brief moment, I thought I had been recognized. Over the loudspeakers, the same smooth voice asks passengers on Flights AF887, AF54 and AF827 to go to boarding Gates 32, 33 and 34. The crowd starts to move. I'm letting myself be pushed along when I see a small red suitcase that's been abandoned. A traveller has also just seen it.

'Is it yours?'

Then everything happens very quickly. I grab it while nodding yes, and head off at a run. Hopefully, no camera has spotted me. But nothing. No one shouts behind me, no one tells me to stop. Leave now. Leave this terminal as quickly as possible. Go to a hotel. Spend the last few euros I have left. Get a room. Breathe.

 CHAPTER 20

From behind the counter, she looks at me, her eyes twinkling.

'If you'd also like a view of the runways, you'll have to go to the Sheraton, but then you'll add a zero to the bill.'

'This will do just fine.'

'How long do you plan to stay?'

'No longer than two hours.'

'Two hours, let's see . . . I have one room left, it's perfect. Are you familiar with our day-use rates? 28 euros for the first hour, 14 euros for each additional hour.'

'Yes, I know.'

'Then, I'll just ask you to pay in advance, please. And here is your key card. The lifts are right behind you.'

IBIS HOTEL

Always more service, always more comfort . . .

I go into the room, making sure that the door shuts firmly behind me. No cameras here, I can finally relax a bit. Is Vlad going to survive? Where am I going to sleep tonight? I have nowhere to go.

I collapse on the bed. Why is it so warm in this room? Have I forgotten what heat is? I turn the thermostat to 0, and stretch out again. But this time, it's the thickness of the mattress that bothers me. How long has it been since I slept in a real bed? And this smell of cleanliness that turns my stomach. Suddenly I'd like to be dirty, dirty like Josias, Liam, Joséphine, to stink, stink like all of them, stop this grotesque charade once and for all, no, I absolutely mustn't think like that, I'm a passenger just about to take off, I pass through security, I'm going home, I fly off and life goes on, but which life, damn it? I shake my head, try to chase away the dark ideas, but how can I not think of Vlad, maybe on his deathbed, and of me in this room, of this way I have of suddenly laughing so bizarrely? Isn't it time to leave everything, to go back to the city, say to the first person I see: 'I don't know who I am, help me!' Several times, I've been tempted to do it, I've even gone so far as to wait for the RER on the platform, but every time, just when I was about to get in, my body refused, as if it knew I was headed to certain death . . . I sit on the ground, lean up against the wall. On the TV I see people talking about war and the massacres they've seen. Sometimes a bit absently, though, but they're there, braving the cameras, telling the world about their misfortunes. Where do they get that courage and why am I so afraid? Is it because I'm really crazy? And yet my fear is real, my fear of the blankness in me which, every night, swallows me whole. Are there others like me? Do they have the same emptiness? I would so like to return to the one I used to be. But when I try to imagine that woman, I turn to ice, as if, out there, everything she did was heartless. So it's better to remain this traveller between two worlds, without name or age. But is that possible? There was yesterday, and the day before yesterday, but yesterday and the day before yesterday there was Vlad, there was Josias, but how about today?

In the shower, I turn the hot water tap on full force. Under the stream of water, I rub my skin until it hurts, that fear, that grime, get rid of all 'that,' take away all 'that' or else become like them. I soap myself twenty times, twenty times I rub shampoo in my hair. At his camp, Vlad protected me. He kept me from them. But what about today when he's no longer there? I increase the temperature as high as it will go. Burn my skin to get clean rather than give up, at least not yet: in the city, there are so many women like me, ready to spout any kind of rubbish to get admitted into a shelter. Who, out there, will believe me, my lost memory, who will protect me? Access to a bed for three days at most, and then, so long lady, you're tossed into the street, a street that rapes you, a street that crushes you—so no, not yet.

The steam is now so thick I can't see the sink. I don't care. Only the power of the water calms me. As if the life in me were demanding it. The life that so needs to find rest, but where? Which world will accept me, this empty body where two—three?—little girls are playing hide-and-seek and where a car flies into the air.

Back in the room, going through the stolen suitcase I discover an array of women's clothes in my size and, in my purse, a badge cord (so that was Liam's present!). I laugh lightly. So many good things, that means I'm going to survive and Vlad is going to get better.

IBIS HOTEL

You're not in a palace, but almost . . .

Hearing the sound of my suitcase rolling on the floor, the girl raises her head.

'So you're leaving?'

'Yes, I'm leaving.'

Clean hair flying in the wind. Washed body, scrubbed, rinsed. Skirt, undershirt, coat, scarf. All new.

The pedestrian crossing to the tourist-bus parking lot where a hundred or so Japanese are taking each other's photos. I take the circular ramp of T1 where I'm grazed by a superb Etihad Airlines A340. A bit farther, a just as beautiful Air Tahiti A340 gets ready on the runway. It looks like the two aeroplanes are sizing each other up. I choke up contemplating the two titans. Over there, the Air Tahiti A340 has come to a halt. Time seems to stand still when, all of a sudden, in an incredible roar, it takes off, bringing everything here along with it. [bringing back? taking along?]

 CHAPTER 21

In the mosque room of the 'ecumenical chapel', a man, his face on the ground, is praying. Opposite, on the Christian side, there is no one. I'm lucky. The silence is so wonderful when no one is here. On the altar covered with a white cloth: a Bible, a lit candle and a cross. I get up and walk over to the book of prayer intercessions that is lying open.

My name is Pierre, I live in Guinee in Conakry, and I ask God to grant me grace to find work to get me out of the mess I'm living in.

All-powerful lord, please make my husband's operation successful.

Thank you, Lord God, for this wonderful vacation.

Lord, I dedicate to you this trip and my daughter who is getting married.

A pen is hanging from a string. I look at it without daring to use it. Did I believe in God before?

On the altar, the little candle flame is flickering. I absolutely don't want it to go out. Quickly, feverishly, I write in the book:

Save Vlad.

 CHAPTER 22

Lucien is the only one I have left here. Seeing how defeated I look, he bombards me with questions. I tell him that at work everyone is stressed out, I'm on the verge of burn-out.

'That's why I left like a thief in the night last time.'

He shrugs his shoulders indulgently.

'Drink your coffee, go on, and come see me when you're done.'

'Are you sure I can come?'

'Sure.'

I hesitate. Why is he so kind to me and who are these 'friends' he wants to introduce me to? When I asked him one day where his generosity came from, he burst out laughing. In his village, everyone has helped each other out since the dawn of time. He doesn't know where that comes from, but he hopes it will continue for ever. What risk am I taking, after all? The night was really hard. I drink my coffee in one gulp, and walk quickly to T2B. At the top of the steps that lead to the lower level, I'm surprised to see travellers turning around and going back the other way. Didn't Lucien ask me to meet him on the lower level? Intrigued, I descend a few steps and suddenly freeze, finding myself in front of an amazing scene: a human sea of people on their knees on prayer rugs, a throng which no one, at that moment, can pass through. Not a centimetre is open. Behind me, a group of tourists are as dumbfounded as I am when they come upon the scene. How many are there? Two hundred? Three hundred? An agent advises travellers to go back the other way. I find myself standing, alone, looking at them all. Without much hope, I try to spot Lucien. I end up sitting down on the stairs, fascinated by the sight of the bodies, an enormous wave rising up that, in a single movement, folds on itself then rises up again before folding, heads bent down to the ground. Is it still the airport here? This carpet of men—which came from where?—unfolding from the entrance to the lost-and-found office to the counters of Hertz and Avis rental-car companies. For twenty minutes I let myself be rocked by the movement of their praying, and then everything fades away. The vision of Vlad's sickly body, that of the burnt camp, of my emptied suitcase.

When Lucien walks up, he's surrounded by two of his 'brothers'. 'A good husband, that's what you need,' he murmurs. Seeing my astonished look, he gestures to his two friends to leave, and sits down beside me.

'I know these men, they're serious and gentle, you have my word.'

'Lucien, I'm really sorry, I'm absolutely not looking to get married.'

With a pensive gesture, he wipes away some invisible dust.

'When I was a child, there was a woman in my village who never left her house. One day, I asked my grandfather about her. He answered: "When one has once been bitten by a snake, one fears the earthworm." '

I look at him, not understanding.

'What does that story have to do with me?'

'I'd bet my life you've been bitten by a terrible snake.'

I turn away.

'You're wrong, Lucien.'

'My cousin said the same thing the day I told him to run away with me. They beat him to death with sticks.'

He doesn't give me time to react, and leans into my ear.

'You don't plan to spend the rest of your life here, do you?'

So he knows. I lower my eyes from the shock. I really want to tell him everything. My fucked-up memory. Vlad's illness. My fear of being arrested. Mistreated. His voice interrupts the flow of my thoughts.

'You still have dreams, don't you?'

'Uh . . . dreams?'

He smiles.

'I arrived in France with nothing. And look at me now. Everyone respects me here. If you focus on your dreams, anything is possible.'

So much goodness. I'm suddenly ashamed. One of his brothers calls to him. He excuses himself, goes over to talk for a few moments. I take advantage to slip away. Just the thought of someone questioning me, even him, Lucien, frightens me. To admit what, and get stuck in which lies? I walk away quickly, heading towards the rolling walkway that connects T2F and T2A-B-C.

'For the hungry children, please, ma'am!'

There are six of them, they are flocking around me, their pens in hand.

'Sign! Here! With your address.'

I escape their circle. A couple behind me isn't as lucky.

Luxury, fashion, beauty, and gourmet food in Duty Free.
Come in, play, and perhaps win
2 diamonds and 10 'must-have' gifts.

The beauty of a light-blue Air France scarf, the clean transparency
of the windows, the synchronization of the Batmen (runway agents
in airport language) on the runways. Behind me, the Romanian
women are dancing around their prey. Their wide smiles and their
skirts.

'You!!???'

I raise my head, and I'm practically nose to nose with the man
with the scarf.

'I've been looking all over for you.'

That smile on his face. My heart clinches. As if it were amusing
to kick a poor girl out! Even before he can raise his hand, I push
him away. Stupefied, he cries out, and almost loses his balance. My
heart is beating wildly. Where can I run now? Behind me, the crowd
is so compact. To the left, then? But to the left the stairs end up at
the VAL platform, a dead end. Without thinking, I run towards the
TGV/RER Station, except he's running after me. Panicked, I drop
my suitcase and run to the escalators. The shouts of travellers I bump
into, quick! I have to move quickly! But his hand grabs me. It's over,
the fight is over. Very slowly, I turn around and face him. For the
second time, he utters this phrase which is actually pretty strange
for a plainclothes cop:

'I've been looking all over for you.'

With a quick glance, I mutely beg him to wait, to let me catch
my breath before he handcuffs me, and he seems to understand,
because he doesn't move. I thank him with my eyes. Most policemen, in these days of terrorist threats, wouldn't have hesitated to

throw me on the ground, shouting. If I were reeking and dirty, I probably would have had more luck. But clean as I am, at this late-morning hour, no, one doesn't just ignore the norms of identification as I have. And now? What place does a woman like me have in the world? Because you need an identity, don't you? Of course, I should have listened to Vlad, but if I had I would have ended up like him. Below ground.

'What's wrong?'

Now I want him to take me away, halt the fear that, standing in front of him, is suffocating me.

'I'm really sorry. I shouldn't have run after you, it was the shock of seeing you again . . . especially today.'

I look up at him again, this time perplexed. A cop would never excuse himself like that.

'*The owner of the red suitcase left in the TGV Station is requested to pick it up as soon as possible.*' In French and English.

'Come on, or they'll explode it.'

He takes my hand.

'Are you coming?'

At the sight of the two soldiers and the security guard on their knees in front of 'my suitcase', I panic. Run away again? But how, when he's pushing me towards them? The guard looks at me, visibly angry.

'It's yours? Right?'

Above all, don't admit it.

'Not even a name tag!'

I still don't respond. He sighs wearily.

'Fine, we'll let it go this time, come on guys, let's get out of here!'

I watch them without understanding. So they're not arresting me? Why did he bring me here, then?

'Catherine had a red suitcase, too.'

I look at him, more and more lost.

'Catherine . . . ?'

'Catherine, my wife.'

' . . . '

'She was on it, you understand?'

' . . . ?'

'On the Rio flight, she was pregnant. That's what she told me right before she took off.'

He swallows a sob.

'You had someone on board, too, didn't you? I've noticed that you've been waiting for someone, I've seen you, haven't I?'

He begs me with his eyes, and suddenly I understand everything. The Rio crash, the loss of his wife . . . He lowers his head.

'I'm at my wits end. Excuse me.' He drops my hand.

'I had someone, yes.'

What came over me to say such a thing? The echo of my answer comes back violently. As if this just invented 'someone' had truly existed, as if, yes, I had lost him as suddenly as he had . . .

'There, breathe slowly . . . lean against me.'

The clicking of the 'Charles de Gaulle' letters. Two flights, from Bamako and Tel Aviv. In the depths of my night, through the streets of those two cities, I walk. Soon, the facades of their buildings will make me dizzy, and that is when I will hear the water. Because the sound of waves can be heard in both. I no longer know which bodies of water. It doesn't matter. The sound of the dust, too. And the magnificent sound of the sand propelled by the wind.

'You need to eat something.'

I let the phrase linger. It's true, he's right: food helps tears.

'The restaurant at the Sheraton, will that be OK? It's very close, and it'll be quiet. It's my treat.'

I smile in spite of myself. The day I arrived, I found myself in front of this ocean liner of a hotel whose windows reflected the ballet of the men on the runways. I have never dared to go in. To sit down in there, without ordering anything, would have quickly aroused suspicions. And now this man is opening its doors for me.

As we walk along, I'm stricken with doubt: lying takes such energy, wouldn't it be better to run away? What am I going to be able to tell him? No one has invited me to lunch before him.

'May I help you?'

Her head comes up from under the counter. She is young, her hair pulled back, white, very elegant. He walks up to her.

'We're here for lunch.'

His voice. A calm voice that reassures me.

'Please follow the hostess, she will be happy to take you to the restaurant.'

We go through a lobby that could be that of a spaceship. In front of a bar, some very concentrated-looking businessmen are talking softly. In the distance, the restaurant is bathed in a soft orange light. The concierge leaves us with a waitress who indicates a quiet table.

'Would you like something to drink?'

He shakes his head, thinking.

'I'll just have a coffee, please.'

'And you, madame?'

This politeness towards me, I'm not used to it.

'. . . uh . . . a gin, please.'

There's a glimmer of surprise in him.

'Never mind the coffee, miss. I'll have a gin, too, that's a great idea.'

I see him smile for the first time.

CHAPTER 23

Sitting on the velvet armchair, my body finally relaxes. The fabric is plush. I sink into it.

'Order whatever you'd like, I'm determined to make it up to you for frightening you the way I did, and also to thank you . . . To thank you for being there.'

I agree with a simple nod, being careful to sit up straight. I'm really afraid that he'll see the amazement I feel in finding myself amid such luxury. Above all, don't look around, take my time reading the menu. Breathe calmly. Act as if I found the situation completely 'normal'.

'Are you ready to order?'

'The beef prix fixe menu, perhaps . . . but what are you going to order?'

'I'll just have the shrimp aspic, but please, feel free.'

I start blushing, mumbling that, unlike most people, emotions make me hungry. Very briefly, his face lights up with a second smile. I breathe. Be careful or he'll detect the lie. Wounded. I am, in his eyes, a wounded woman who is unable to overcome her grief. The waitress reappears.

'Here are your two gins.'

He stares absently at his glass, as if it is bringing back an old memory, then he raises it. I'm about to do the same when, suddenly, he starts talking to me, rapidly, as if, after months of silence, he finally has the opportunity to open up.

'Catherine is an excellent swimmer. She even won prizes when she was young. We met in a swimming pool. We banged heads. She was doing the backstroke, and I the breaststroke. I immediately loved her eyes.'

'Catherine, your . . . wife?'

'My wife, yes.'

'But you had said she was . . . I mean, you are talking about her as if she . . .'

'I'm sorry, I sometimes forget to use the past tense.'

He shakes his head, lost.

'In the beginning, I accepted what they told me. You remember, the little room where they gathered us all? Then I suddenly needed to get outside. Less than a metre away, a woman was struggling to get her suitcase out of the trunk of her car. Mine was dead, I had just been informed, and, with her, more than two hundred other people. Cars were coming and going, people were unloading their baggage, she was dead, I had just been informed, a guy was shouting not to be late, others, with enormous bags, were hugging and kissing, meeting again, in the same place where I had helped her carry her suitcase, it was devastating. I stayed there a few minutes, until some-one came to get me. He had seen me go out. "Come on, you can't stay like that." He, too, was crying, he didn't have anyone in the plane, but he worked here, and for them, when a plane crashes, it's like a part of themselves disappears, that's what he said, I'll never forget. Afterwards, I thought I would mourn. But, one morning, I got up, and I came here, in front of the Arrivals doors. It felt so good to wait again! You're the only one who can understand me. The doors open. She arrives. I can see her coming towards me. She's smiling wearing her blue coat, the one I bought for her in Italy. It was cold, raining, we hadn't planned on the bad weather. When I showed her the coat in a store window, she smiled. It was incredibly expensive. So I went in. She thought I was bluffing. She laughed. We were always playing jokes on each other. Then I reappeared with the coat. Just the coat. No bag. "No, you didn't do it!" She couldn't believe it! It was blue. Light blue like her eyes.'

He falls silent, turns his head to avoid my eyes.

'I'm only talking about myself, I'm sorry . . .'

Now I have to say something. I can't leave him like that. I lower my eyes, stroke the thick, white fabric of the tablecloth . . .

'I . . . I lived with him in a large house.'

'Was he your husband?'

I freeze, make a superhuman effort to contain my panic.

'The fridge was always full. We ate a tonne of vegetables.'

'. . . vegetables?'

'Sorry, I . . . I have to go. I'm talking nonsense.'

He takes my hand, holding me back. Pain has also shattered him. He understands everything, even the suitcase. A suitcase has nothing to do with it. One doesn't wait with a suitcase. But he understands why I do.

'One day, the doors will open and we will disappear behind them.'

I look at him, disconcerted. That sentence means absolutely nothing. Am I dealing with a madman? He carries on talking as if nothing were the matter.

'Sometimes, I tell myself that they are on an island waiting for us and . . .'

He stops in mid-sentence, then looks straight at me.

'I'm frightening you.'

I start to say something, but he doesn't give me time.

'Everywhere I go I see her. It's crazy. It's been years since she's been gone. I should have gone through mourning a long time ago. To tell you the truth, I don't understand myself what makes me so . . . obsessed. I've talked to shrinks . . . Just imagine. Even today I can't bring myself to throw out her things. Everything in the closets is still there: her creams, her dresses, her trinkets. My family, understandably, has lost patience. I've created a void around me . . .'

He picks up his jacket, gets ready to stand up.

'I'm really sorry, I won't bother you any more.'

I take his hand.

'Please, don't leave.'

The begging in my voice. He looks at me, surprised. But how can I tell him that I don't have a euro on me, and that, after the night I've just spent, I really need to eat if I don't want to have a spell that will lead directly to expulsion. In addition, his story is moving, as if it is awakening something in me I don't know, something that . . .

'You were going to say something.'

His voice, once again so soft. I close my eyes, let his words flow over me: there are so many things he doesn't know. Not the circumstances of the accident, nor what it was like on the plane itself: everyone received a lot of information, but no words can replace a body. A living body, that is. Careful, I'm not about to tell him that they are alive. To tell the truth, I don't know anything about it. Dead.

Alive. They are floating somewhere in infinite space. So many things he doesn't know. This encounter between him and me, for example, while Vlad is probably dying in a hospital corridor and Josias, mad with jealousy, is screaming my name through the parking lot of the second sub-basement of T2A, but how can I talk about 'that'? He looks at me, puzzled.

'This meeting between us, it's true . . . I mean, precisely today, when I had decided to . . .'

'To what?'

'No, nothing . . . I'm sorry.'

That fragility in his voice.

'You were going to kill yourself?'

He looks at me without speaking. How could I have guessed? But to answer that I would have to tell him about Vlad, the same desire to end it all deep in his eyes.

'Is that it?'

He lowers his head.

'Yes.'

I scarcely hear him. I rest my hand on his.

'My name is Anna, what's yours?'

This way I have of shaking him up. Of waking him up. He looks at me with his sad eyes.

'Luc.'

The waitress reappears.

'I forgot to tell you that for dessert today we have our home-made crepes: chocolate, apricot, honey lemon, caramel. All the profits from sales will be used for the victims' families in the Philippines.'

'Something happened in the Philippines?'

She looks at me, astonished.

'You don't know about the horrible flooding?'

Eight days stuck underground . . . Even he seems surprised.

'You didn't understand me . . . I meant . . . something has happened there *again*?'

A release of tension.

'Thank God, no. They've had their share of death.'

I agree in silence. I could have caused a scandal. Never forget to follow the rules:

Control the body. Contain the body.

Serious behaviour. Serious demeanour. Never leave tracks: throw cigarette butts in bins, throw garbage in bins. No excessive gestures. Scratch, but not to the point of bleeding. Drink, but not out of the bottle. Run, no. Shout, no. Stick to the codes. To the limits. To the procedures. And for me, who speaks to others: *always know current events.*

I turn towards the waitress.

'I'll have an apricot crepe instead of the chocolate.'

'Excellent, madame. And for you, sir?'

'I'm really not hungry, I'm sorry.'

She walks away. He tells me it's good, what they're doing for those poor people, wonders what will become of them. Basically, he would have liked to have been there when the rising waters caused the landslides: he would have let himself be swallowed up. I stop him with a gesture.

'When one really dies, one shouts.'

He looks at me again, surprised, wondering if he heard right. I finish my meal in silence.

BEING OPEN TO THE WORLD IS TO UNDERSTAND DIFFERENCES. HSBC, YOUR BANK, EVERYWHERE IN THE WORLD.

Going along the rolling walkway that leads to T2E, he offers to give me a ride home.

'I've parked at T2B.'

How can I respond? This purse isn't mine. This suitcase isn't mine. Nor do I have a name (I've just invented Anna), or address. I don't even know where or in what year I was born. Following a shock—an attack? An accident?—I've lost everything about my past except for a few snippets when I see the little girls run, the face of a man, a car accident . . . Are they my daughters? And that man, is he my husband? Were they all in the car when . . . The more I try to remember, the more my anguish grows, as if that woman I had been was hiding the worst. But what? It was here, in this airport, that eight months ago I regained consciousness. Here, where I like everything, even the sound the wind makes through the doors, the cleanliness of the trashcans, the energy of the travellers, their way of turning towards the windows when the A380 takes off, Vlad, Josias, and even him, Luc, right now, so broken, who is looking at me.

'Do you live in Paris?'

Why is he insisting?

'No.'

'So, in the suburbs?'

Should I shout at him? I don't have a flat or a job or a car, I live here and no one, not even he, will take me somewhere else.

'I can make a detour if you'd like.'

Don't give in to the desire to run away, leaving him standing here. I lower my eyes, take a deep breath.

'I'll get home by myself, thank you.'

He doesn't move. He needs to leave now, he and his questions that take me back to all that I've lost, he needs to disappear! But no, he insists on seeing me again.

'Tomorrow, ten o'clock, in front of Arrivals.'

He raises his hand and I think it's to shake mine. Instead, before leaving, he simply readjusts the collar of my sweater. A gesture that overwhelms me though I don't understand why.

CHAPTER 24

I stand for a long time in front of the moving walkway, not moving.

'Do you need any help?'

It's a young couple, glowing.

'Help?'

The girl takes out a pack of Kleenex.

'You're crying.'

Crying? I bring my hand up to my face, feel the tears running down my cheeks. They're standing in front of me, smiling.

'We're on our way to Ile Maurice, we're on our honeymoon!'

They laugh, and their laughter enters into me. She opens her suitcase.

'I'm going to give you a piece of my wedding veil, I brought it with us. I can't leave you like this!'

She finds it under a pile of clothes, tears off a piece, and hands it to me.

'There—now nothing bad will ever happen to you!'

They're not drunk, just filled to the brim with joy. They run off before I have a chance to thank them.

 CHAPTER 25

Terminal 2B. Numb. Sitting for how long? Behind the glass, opposite the moving baggage belts, bunches of men and women looking for their luggage. Alone or in little groups they leave, their hands gripping the handles of their carts, holding on to what? I'd like to get up, walk towards them. Instead, Vlad's lost look, the double doors of the EMS, the vandalized camp, keep coming back to me. To calm myself I try to concentrate on the music of the various languages, the scent of bodies. But it takes just one oddity within the crowd and the disorder shatters me all over again.

'Would you mind holding my sign while I go outside for a smoke? I've been waiting for my client for more than an hour. I won't be long. Do you mind? Thanks, really.'

MADAME LINHART / SOCIÉTÉ DBM

What if I've made everything up? If none of them really exist? Vlad? Josias? Lucien? Liam? What if they are only a part of myself, a pure creation of my addled brain, the debris of intense emotions, buried, hidden? Me, this woman sitting at this meeting place, in this terminal whose smallest details I know, an abyss where, in the greatest disorder, every language, every time and space are mixed together, me, this airport, otherwise death? In some books, life is prolonged, identical to this one, I read that somewhere. Or nothing of the kind, a series of events that, since the beginning, without any apparent logic, have befallen me.

'You have a new suitcase now!'

I let out a cry when I see him.

'Josias?'

He's shaking all over, reeks of alcohol, eyes me with his mean look.

'My mother is right, you fuck everything up! Who did you steal this one from?'

I stand up, horrified.

'Josias, please . . .'

He blocks my path.

'You don't give a shit about me, do you? You only care about your Vlad!'

Some travellers turn around. I need to act fast before the security guards intervene.

'I swear that . . .'

'What if I tell you that he's dead, then what?'

I look at him, crushed.

'He's not dead, you're lying.'

'Go see Carlion if you don't believe me!'

Such hatred on his face. A dull anger rises up in me.

'Fine, I will.'

'He won't tell you anything.'

'I'll tell him everything, he'll tell me.'

He continues to block my path.

'He won't tell you anything, I'm telling you!'

I shove him aside, hand the sign to an astonished onlooker who watches me rush away.

The VAL platform. Arrival of the VAL.

For your safety, hold on to the handrail.

I go into the first train carriage. Josias, who has followed me, is right behind, muttering behind my back that, since my appearance the other night, Joséphine hasn't spoken a word to him.

'How many times have I told you to never show up. In her head, we are hers, Liam and me, only hers. Shit, what am I going to do now? Are you listening to me?'

I turn towards him, glaring.

'*Your* Russians destroyed everything at Vlad's camp.'

The blow falls. He lowers his eyes.

'They almost got me, too. Are you happy?'

His silence says it all. He clenches his fists, his eyes fill with tears.

'OK, you win. He's not dead.'

He's angry at himself for having gone that far. He loves me, he adds quietly . . . Can I understand that, he loves me? I nod, ask him if Vlad's going to be OK. He seems mad again, lets it go, then mumbles yes. He's shaking. He's drunk on love, drunk on jealousy.

'I didn't want the Russians to hurt you.'

'What about the money?'

'I owed it to them.'

'What's Vlad going to do?'

'He'll get by.'

'That's rotten.'

'Because you think he's squeaky clean? You should have seen how Carlion reacted when he saw him.'

★

'Is Vlad the name he gave you?'

'Vlad, yes, Doctor.'

'On the side of the lifts in T2C, right?'

'Yes.'

'What floor?'

'Level -1, I already told you.'

'That's all?'

'What do you mean, that's all?'

'What about the rest, you know, yes or no?'

'What rest, which rest?'

'What he's done, did he tell you, yes or no, damn it?'

'How am I supposed to know!'

'All the better for you, Josias, because it's not very pretty! Go on, get out of here, I need to take care of him now.'

★

'You're still lying! No one knew he was there.'

'That's right, blame me again! You're just like all the rest!'

The doors open. He goes away, stumbling.

'Nothing but a dirty, stinking whore!'

A group of Japanese smile at me. Upset, I turn around, go find a seat at the front. All the love that trembles in me and which, every time, has failed, as if a part of me were relentlessly trying to destroy everything. What sort of woman have I been? Rather, what kind of monster? I curl up on my seat. With Vlad, that virus situation should have been obvious. But I didn't notice anything.

CHAPTER 26

It's snowing outside. The dance of the Boschungs on the runways. Impossible to sleep. Around 4 a.m. I lie down next to a family that has put blankets on the ground. I don't have anything, but I'm so tired it doesn't matter. A man's voice awakens me. A tall Black man, broom in hand, explains that I can't sleep on the ground like that. Outside, it's not yet daybreak, but already the first travellers are streaming in. They all look at me, surprised. How could I have slept there? The tall Black man sighs. I slip away without even trying to explain myself.

The women's room in 2F. Icy water on my face. But the nightmare persists. It doesn't want to go away. I'm walking in a deserted city. In the distance I see a large crack opening up, rushing towards me. Terrified, I start to run, trying to avoid the blocks of stone that, under its terrifying push, are falling off buildings. Where is everyone, and why can't I hear anything? On the ground, in front and behind me, dozens of gaps appear, forming a huge maze. Increasingly panicked, I zigzag in every direction. How long will I be able to hold out and, above all, where can I find a safe place in the middle of this chaos? Then, right in front of me, a woman and a little girl, from the back, not moving. Don't they see that the city is collapsing? Why aren't they running? I start screaming at them to run, but nothing, not a movement, as if they didn't hear me. So I run towards them, and just when I reach them, horror! The woman's face is mine! I look at her, stunned, screaming that they have to leave. But instead of doing what I tell her, she grabs me and forces me to watch the crevasse that is coming straight at us. I beg her to let me go. What have I done to her to deserve this? And what about her little girl, has she thought of her? Too late. The ground under our feet disappears and, just as we're falling, I scream so loudly that sometimes the scream awakens me with a start.

Where am I? And why isn't Vlad by my side? Then everything comes back, and it's as if I am being thrown a second time into that gaping hole. Lost, I stare at my reflection in the mirror. Without Vlad I feel so vulnerable. His harshness forced me to react. I turn around at the sound of footsteps. She's around thirty, has brown, smiling eyes.

'So you're going to Madagascar like that?'

I look at her, uncomfortable.

'Uh . . . . No, why?'

'Because of the sticker on your suitcase. I live there. Have you ever been?'

Keep improvising over and over. Keep my head above water.

'Not I, no, but . . . a friend loaned me her suitcase.'

'Do you live in Paris?'

'Yes, in Paris.'

'I'm spending the holidays with my sister. She lives in Lille. Where are you headed?'

In my head, the information is dancing.

'To . . . Lithuania. My brother is stationed there.'

'Brrr . . . it must be colder than here! I hope you've brought what you need.'

'Yes, I have.'

She leaves. My head is spinning. That flood of questions. I rest my hands on the rim of the sink to get hold of myself.

'Come here! Come here, I've found something!' shouts the little girl, perched on the rim of a well.

Then everything moves very quickly. Her light little laugh facing the black void she's leaning over. Her body which suddenly moves . . . disappears! Then silence in the garden, followed by a thud! I stay a few seconds, my eyes riveted on the void: Élodie? Almost tripping with every step, I manage to back away through the tall grass until I feel my strength draining out of me. Farther away, in the house, I'm crushing nuts. A man's voice behind me. Tired.

'This can't go on.'

I'm not listening to him, I stuff a handful of nuts into my mouth, crunch them, and feel all my teeth shatter.

When I open my eyes again, I'm on the ground. Blinded by the overhead lights, I get up slowly. Luckily, no one has come in. I lean over the sink, dizzy. That . . . little girl who fell in the well? In the mirror, my body is leaning, and it's as if it is repeating what it did back there, staring, petrified, at the bottom of the well. I can still hear the horrible thud. I turn the cold water tap on full force. That horrible noise the nuts made in my mouth. Had I really done that? No, impossible. I still have all my teeth.

Oh, how I would suddenly like to collapse in the tall grass. *Forget everything.*

(edited)

He told them that He didn't discriminate against anyone and that He wasn't there to sow hatred. They didn't seem to understand Him, they even got mad, asking Him clearly to stop saying any old thing. He then told Himself that they were playing their roles perfectly, because they truly seemed surprised. However, whereas He was continuing to talk to them about the little girl found dead in her parents' closet at the very moment when most claimed they were ready to pay to LEARN ENGLISH WHILE LAUGHING, which—by the way—is of HORRIBLE seriousness, they suddenly released Him, REFUSING to hear ANY MORE about it, whereas they should have MADE A SIGN to Him—in other words, how could the Letters give themselves the DATE OF THE GREAT GATHERING? But, instead of continuing to play their roles to finally GIVE HIM THE MEANS TO REVEAL THE GREAT SECRET TO THEM, they all turned their backs on Him, but THEY ALL wore Letters, which indicates how serious the hour is, how much, even, EVERYTHING IS PERHAPS ALREADY LOST.

MOREOVER, YESTERDAY, ON THE TELEVISION, HE SAW THE EXTRAORDINARY PERFORMANCE OF THE NEW SUITCASES capable of going up and down stairs! As if they were going to need to climb and go down STAIRS when they arrive OVER THERE! But ALL THOSE WHO WATCHED the television seemed to approve, some even going so far as to say that with such suitcases they felt ready to treat themselves to a relaxing weekend at an oriental spa, a weekend from which NO ONE returned, He is in a good position to know! BECAUSE OF THEM, of the FRIGHTENING example they set, more and more men and women and children LEAVE, bringing behind them ENTIRE

POPULATIONS that, under His eyes as POWERLESS SON, jump into aeroplanes which, they think, are taking them to their Well-Being destinations where each one can treat himself to TRENDY DINNERS whereas In Truth, THEY ALL are headed towards the TEN DESTINATIONS FOR 1,000 EUROS so that not one single man with a degree will any longer ever be able to find a job, so that the poison of chemical factories spreads into women's milk, and that the COMING AND GOING OF THE FLOW AND THE REFLOW FINISHES THEM ALL OFF, and this, despite the number of LETTERS that, around him, continues to grow, but WHO among them henceforth believes and why does the snow insist on falling? Whatever happened to HUGO BOSS? IS THE END ALREADY HERE?

 CHAPTER 27

Outside, daylight is just beginning to appear. I find a newspaper on a seat, thumb through it, exhausted. I'm struggling to keep my eyes open on the headlines when a shout interrupts my reading.

'Son-stealer! Ogress!'

Stunned, I see Joséphine pointing at me.

'She's lying to you! She's an impostor! She never travels!'

I stare at her, incapable of responding. She comes closer, full of hate, and is about to strike me when three guards descend upon her, while a fourth, accompanied by a dog, sits next to me, telling me not to be afraid. Over there, they haul away Joséphine who is fighting and spitting insults at them.

Anthony (badge) stays with me, and shows me his dog.

'Her name is Ilka, you can pet her if you want. There, there, on top of her head, she's really very gentle.'

'Thank you, I need to go now.'

'Catch your breath. You're only five minutes from the gates, right? She won't return, relax.'

'I think I'd like to get some fresh air, outside.'

'OK, but I'll go with you.'

He's thirty-two, Ilka has been living with him for ten years. She received special training to sniff out explosives. It's rare that they walk around the terminals together. Usually they're in the baggage-sorting area, a place off-limits to travellers.

'You'd be amazed, it's a huge hangar, there are conveyor belts everywhere with suitcases moving in all directions. They come, they go, everything is regimented as if it were a musical score. Even after all these years, it continues to amaze me. All those belts that inter-twine up to the ceiling! Is a suitcase too early? It is placed on one of the holding platforms. Is a suitcase too late? When it goes by, all the belts stop. When I let Ilka loose on those mountains of luggage, I give her lots of encouragement. It helps her when she hears me tell her she's beautiful, that I'm proud of her. She couldn't do it, otherwise. There are too many. Really too many. When she stops and looks at me, that means she's found something. I then get up on the belt and check it out.'

'Have you ever found a bomb?'

'No, but a shell, a couple months ago.'

'A shell?'

'Some guy had found it in his yard and wanted to show it to his American friends. For that discovery, believe me, I gave my girl a really nice reward! Right, Ilka? Do you remember?'

He rubs his dog's head and says he's happy he made me laugh.

'Feeling better now?'

'Yes, thank you.'

'With everything going on in the world, it's good to talk a bit, isn't it?'

He stands up, and walks away.

Outside, the snow has stopped falling.

LE PAVILLON DE RÉCEPTION DES CHEFS D'ETAT

A lounge and conference room for heads of state.

There are 1,500 flags in the basement. As for the red carpet that connects the pavilion to the runway, there are two choices of length: 40 metres or 120 metres.

 CHAPTER 28

9.45 a.m.: I who, yesterday, didn't expect to see him again, am now in front of the 16 Arrival doors, hoping with all my strength to see him. The nightmare of last night, and the attack by Joséphine this morning . . . Wait for him so I don't implode, or go out, retrace my steps, sit down, get up, push the doors, wander around, take the lifts, go in circles. My mouth is so dry this morning. I've reached my limit.

Landing of flights from Boston; Chicago; Santiago, Chile; Edinburgh . . .

A DUTY FREE SHOP LIKE NONE OTHER

10 a.m. Arrival of the Rio–Paris flight: still no trace of him. Standing next to me, some staff are talking about the theft last night of two multicoloured cows that were placed at the entrance to the airport.

Mathias (badge) rolls his eyes.

'Stealing things like that, really?!'

They both start laughing. I stare at them, exhausted.

'Hey, that lady looks really funny . . .'

I'm about to answer them, when a violent torrent of images rises up in me. One of the men stares at me, looking concerned.

'Would you like to sit down?'

Clench my fists, turn my back to him before he . . . start running, bumping into, here, a traveller who curses me, there, another who shouts. Anything to avoid being invaded by this chaos, or else I . . .

'Anna!'

Luc, his face sweaty, looks at me, sputtering his apologies. That blue coat he noticed in the crowd, he thought he recognized it, ran after it, he wanted . . . he no longer really knows what he wants any more. He holds me against him.

'Anna, do something, I'm going crazy.'

The weight of his hands on me, the density of his sorrow. When he touches me, the surging memories dissipate as abruptly as they had emerged and I freeze for a moment from the shock. I, too, need to catch my breath. I have an idea.

'Did you come by car?'

He answers yes, dazed.

'Where are you parked?'

'In the 2B parking lot.'

'Come on, a little air will do us good.'

He leads me to the third sub-level, points his key at a grey Laguna, and we drive off without saying a word. At the exit, I ask him to go left. We go through the freight zone, reach a roundabout and I direct him to exit on to a small road. Some five hundred metres farther, beyond the abandoned bridge, I point out the N17 highway below. Seen from here, the number of large trucks and cars seems unreal. We drive a bit further and, just before the road ends, I ask him to park, on the right, against the embankment.

'Here? You're sure?'

I nod yes and, barely out of the car, I start climbing, and he has no choice but to follow me. The crunching of our steps in the snow continues, then we hear a thundering that causes him to cry out: the gigantic shadow of a Boeing 747 that in an instant grazes our heads and plunges us into darkness. At a run, I reach the fence that borders the end of the runway, and flatten my body against it.

'Come on, Luc!'

But, petrified, he doesn't move. In a deafening roar, the plane gets ready to touch down. I turn around, shout at him again to join me. He has to see this, hear this, that precise moment when the wheels, in a deafening din, strike the ground completely and when the earth under your feet trembles, an explosion, the fury of the world, the earth, our bodies, the pain of our bodies, stricken, riven, brakes, the screeching of brakes, waves of snow that rise up in every direction. How I love it, this furious tumult, and he, as if mesmerized, finally moves forward, clutches the fence and begins shouting her name: Catherine! While at the end of the runway, in a roaring that doesn't end, the Boeing disappears in an eddy of ice.

Without looking at each other, we hold our breaths. In less than a minute, a second plane will appear, then a third, a fourth, and each time, the same sensation of succumbing underneath it, of being resurrected underneath it. Redoubtable gods that, one after the other, have been crushing us, pulverizing us, saving us, for how long? I look at my frozen fingers on the fence, it is so good to be cold, to shiver from head to toe, life finally returned, a sensation of being here. I glance over at Luc who is looking at me. Staring, really. Is it because he's angry? But maybe he's cold, too, and simply wants to return to the car. Without taking his eyes off me, he walks towards me and suddenly embraces me, muttering thanks. I want to stay like this for ever. It has been so long since I've been embraced like this.

Inside, though, something is contracting. Something that can't tolerate the emergence of new happiness.

'*You don't want to, is that it?*'

    The exasperated look he gives me. Luc or that man, in that house, who insists I allow him to make love to me? The harshness of my answer.

    'I don't want to, that's all.'

    Outside, a light rain is running down the car windows. His weariness next to me. You never want to. I laugh, at least I believe I hear myself laugh at the very moment when everything in me wants to cry. Where am I? Above my body, a quiet voice begs me to stay calm. Yours, Luc? All these walls of sadness that don't want to come down. I must open the door, I must leave, but the man catches me. You're my wife, damn it. Skirt raised under his caresses, I pull it back down brusquely. Leave me alone! So harsh, my voice, so implacable. The man, my husband, Marc! Yes, it was Marc, everything is coming back! Marc in his real-estate agent suit, his rage gone, if you knew how sick I am of your coldness. And I of your mistresses! And now, that road where, under a deluge of rain, I'm driving. On the radio, an old song, I sing along. Is it the same day? A bend in the road coming up. The refrain returns and I sing a bit louder as if I'm addressing someone I love. And yet there's no one next to me, and behind me . . . but why do I stiffen, and why does my gaze become so fixed, what's come over me, WHY AM I SWERVING?

    The car, at full speed, spins around, strikes the edge, flies off. The height of the trees, did you know that? But who are you, whose face I am desperately looking for and who implores me to . . . Too late, the car is turning around in the air. Get it to come down, I'd like to, and I try, I swear, so loving that voice, so strangely calm, whereas the car, at a speed I didn't think possible, slams right into a tree trunk, the sound of windows exploding, my head, my body, my . . .

'Anna, are you all right?'

What made me swerve like that?

'Anna ...'

I open my eyes, drenched in sweat. That voice I thought I heard in the car ... Élodie, the little girl at the well? Is she the one I killed? But what about her sister? And the well? I shake my head, I'm lost.

'Anna, at least let me take you home.'

'Home' ... I hear that word like a slap. When will he understand? In a terrible grinding an Etihad aeroplane skims over our heads.

'Anna, say something ...'

Was I trying to kill myself? What about Marc? Wouldn't it rather be he I ...

'Anna, please, look at me.'

And he, Luc, with his questions, his shaved face and his apartment, he whom I want to flee, so handsome just a moment ago shouting out his pain, why can't I do it? Is it because I ...

'Then let's go to a hotel ...'

I look at him without understanding.

'Just to rest, Anna, nothing more. I'm exhausted, too.'

 CHAPTER 29

When he parks in front of the Hilton, my heart races. Here, they'll undoubtedly ask for some identification! How could I have agreed to this?! I'm about to ask him to turn around. Too late. A valet opens my door.

Going through the huge marble-covered lobby, whose luxury only increases my anxiety. Moving towards the Reception, I turn and go sit down in an armchair, pretending I don't feel well. A few metres away, I see Luc checking us in. Whom did he say I was? His partner? His wife?

'Anna, do you feel well enough to stand up?'

That calm which exudes from him and wounds me as much as it reassures me. What force is pushing me to follow him like this? His pain is so clear. At his side, I feel intangible, a blur. We go into one of the three glass-walled lifts which, under a glass ceiling, come and go along the atrium. At our feet, the customers at the bar become small dots, and I again wonder if all of this is a dream. In the room on the eighth floor, the window opens onto the Concorde. Wouldn't I be better off over there, rather than pretending to be a normal woman in this room where, already, I'm suffocating?

Vlad, where are you? And you, Josias? Suddenly, I want to see them, excuse myself for being here, among those who hate them.

'Anna?'

What does he want, in fact? To sleep together, is that it? He smiles sadly. No, Anna, just to rest beside you. I mutter an excuse, feeling ill at ease. It's so strange to find myself in this room, with him. He shakes his head, says that since the crash, we are like two broken children. At that moment I want to tell him that I've been lying about everything, to admit that I didn't lose anyone on that flight. I stare at the ground, silent.

'Anna, you're trembling.'

'It's that word, broken.'

He stares into my eyes. This emotion between us. This desire that surprises me. He closes his eyes, brushes my lips with his hand. That pain he holds out to me. So heavy, so full of memories. So many blue coats here. One might even call it an adieu. Tears are rolling down his cheeks, his fingers enlace mine, caress my face. There have never been any dead. No plane went down. I am Catherine, his wife, and how wonderful it is to imagine the flat where, soon, he will help me unpack my suitcase and where we'll make love. We slowly move towards the bed. Our bodies come closer, almost stuck together. Our kisses become increasingly passionate, but, suddenly, he pulls away.

'No, I can't.'

I pull him to me. He turns away, clearly at a loss.

'I'm sorry. I never should have . . .'

In the distance, at the end of the runway, a Gulf Air is taking off. He stands up, takes his coat.

'Come on, Anna, I'll take you home.'

But I want to stay here. With him.

'Anna, it's impossible.'

He's right, it's impossible. I'd like to shout it out at him. As if someone could be attracted by a woman who deliberately drives into a tree and who kills, because I've killed, haven't I? Behind me, I hear the sound of the door closing. I stay for a long time curled up, not moving, then I suddenly notice a reflection in the mirror, a body that takes me some time to recognize: me, that curled up woman I'm pointing at. Look! She seems to be begging me, look even more deeply: before the tree, before the spectacular whiteness of the tree, it's there, in the void, that you must . . .

Dig down, lose everything.

The car strikes the edge of the road, I am the wife of Marc, a real-estate agent who wants to make love to me, and to whom I say no. What happened to him after the accident? And why didn't they take me back home? Did that big house ever exist? And that voice in the car, begging me? That voice I would so love to hear again? In the mirror, the reflection is silent, and the pain is overwhelming.

CHAPTER 30

How long did I stay motionless facing the wall last night? In my head, the words stopped coming, or were cut off. It sounded like yelping. It is time to leave here and get back to my new world. The only one where I can still stand up straight.

In front of the hotel, the doorman suggests that I wait for the shuttle that goes around the terminals. I tell him I prefer to walk. The snow everywhere is so beautiful. I decide to cut through the fields. Except that soon my feet sink so deeply that I can't continue. My eyes looking up at the sky, I lay down to catch my breath. To melt into the landscape, that's what I want to do this morning. Become as fluid as the air. And blue. Entirely blue like the sky. I'm surprised to find I'm smiling. What do I have to be afraid of, after all? All I have to do is go back to Vlad's camp and fix it up again, pick up my life from before until one fine morning Vlad returns. But something doesn't feel right. Something hints at an unfathomable void. Him, Luc?

Draw a circle in the snow. Sit down in the centre. Build a transparent wall all around and stay there, never moving or feeling anything again, because feeling is too violent here. In the meanwhile, the world will burn. It is burning, by the way, except I don't remember. Rest my chin on my knees, draw a second circle, inside myself, this time, take everything out of it, enter the void where the planes, the men, the little girls, the eyes of the guards, the shouting, soundless, spin around. Finally, don't think about anything at all, not even about those who, at that moment, are in front of the security gates, emptying their pockets, meekly, and taking off their shoes. Hug your knees. Extinguish all screens. No longer see or listen to anything. Plunge inside that silence where aeroplanes never crash, houses never disappear, and into which I am now sinking . . .

★

Is it because of the snowflake she swallowed? Some say they saw her tilt her head back and gulp it down. It was snowing that day. The children were having fun throwing snowballs at cars while, behind the windows, she still wasn't moving. Which war, at that time, was being threatened? Those who came to see her weren't thinking of that. They stopped to look at her, and it was as if a part of themselves were conversing with her. About what, they didn't know. The windows were so high and she seemed so fragile inside. Perhaps about the adolescent whose remains had been found on the rails and who, they said, had committed suicide because of a banal love story, but perhaps about their fear of unemployment, their desire for holidays, or about their cat, also about their need for love and security. Is it because they were absorbed in their thoughts that they didn't see it? From what some very rare people said, suddenly the windows disappeared. It was a man who had performed that miracle. A man on whose face one could read a huge sadness. How had he performed that feat? When he approached, the little girl had trembled. Was it he whom she was waiting for? He who, with infinite gentleness, is now leaning over her. But who, he? And who, she? While the children throw snowballs as hard as they can and, behind the windows, she shudders.

★

I slowly open my eyes, and, amazed, see Luc covering me with his coat and vigorously rubbing my back.

'Anna, this is pure madness! To lay down in the snow in such cold!'

How did he find me?

'All morning I've been watching for you to come out of the hotel. I don't know how I could have missed you, probably when I dozed off. The doorman told me you had left on foot . . . I wanted to apologize for last night.'

But I don't want anything any more. Snow. Just contact with the snow.

'I beg of you, Anna, I need you . . .'

That fracture in him, the sky all around, the snow like fire. He hugs me again. I allow myself to be enwrapped.

In the car, my teeth are chattering. Without saying anything, he starts the car and turns up the heat as high as it will go. He probably wants me to talk about myself. Who are you, Anna? Where do you live? What do you do in life? I would then have to tell him about that room where I woke up without any memory, of that little girl who falls, of that car that flies into the air, of the planes that have saved me . . . Instead, I point out in the distance the oil tanks of Épinay-les-Louves connected by a pipeline to Le Havre which, every day, deliver all the fuel needed for the planes: no less than 15,000 gallons. He's surprised that I should know such a thing, but doesn't question me. Vlad would have yelled, and Josias would have whistled in admiration, but he's not one of 'those people'.

CLUB LOOKÉA
Memories guaranteed!

134

I follow him on the moving walkways of the departure level of TC2, my head lowered. Fingers crossed that neither Joséphine nor Josias appear! Finally, he stops in front of Brasserie Paul and I breathe. None of them would dare come in here. Anxiety, though, when he raises his hand to call over the waitress, suggesting I order the complete breakfast. With hardly 2 euros on me, I can't even afford an espresso. He must sense my discomfort.

'My treat.'

Angela (badge), a slight Italian accent, writes down the order, a smile on her lips.

'To confirm: two full breakfasts, one with a double espresso, the other with hot chocolate.'

'That's right, thank you.'

She's about to turn around when she sees my little suitcase.

'So you're going on vacation with that?'

I nod my head yes.

'You're lucky, where are you going?'

The old habits kick in.

'To Morocco.'

'To the sun, I would have guessed! Have you ever been there?'

I respond without thinking.

'We've just bought a riad in Marrakech and plan to move there when our eldest is old enough to be on his own.'

Angela starts laughing. She, too, has promised herself to go back to Sicily with her husband to open a restaurant.

'But, of course, we can't leave France until the youngest has passed the Bac!'

She walks away.

'Do you ... do that often?'

Good lord, I had almost forgotten him!

'When I'm not feeling well, I ... yes ... it takes my mind off things ...'

As we're about to part ways, he offers to take me home. I refuse, claiming I need to be alone. He insists: public transportation isn't very reliable with all this snow. I tell him he needn't worry, I'm used to it. He would have probably liked to prolong the moment, but time is passing quickly and I have to find a place to sleep.

When I arrive at T1, I take the service stairs to the first sub-level. With a firm stride, I walk through the underground corridors, suddenly hoping I'll find Vlad. When I reach the campsite, my enthusiasm dissipates: not only have all his things disappeared, but the ground is covered with water, which makes any camping impossible, even for one night. Who could have done that? The firemen? The Russians? Even the mattress has disappeared! Leaning against the damp wall, I try not to cry. Where am I going to sleep, and what will Vlad do when he returns? When I go back to the terminals, wandering, I start to miss Luc again, Luc with his serious air, the loss in his eyes.

'Excuse me, do you know how these things work, the self-service kiosks?'

He must be eighty. He talks with a slight Spanish accent.

'All these electronic gadgets! Frankly, it was better before, wasn't it?'

Before, I don't know. Neither Luc nor Vlad existed.

The planes flew. I didn't watch them.

Terminal 2F. Standing in front of the crowd milling around, some sitting on the ground, I bless the snow. Most flights are showing lengthy delays. Impossible to be noticed by anyone in this chaos.

With each new announcement, all eyes turn to the screens. I seize the opportunity to grab a scarf here, a sweater there, a sandwich there, too. Never have the pickings been as bountiful or as good.

It is past 10 when I fall asleep among a dozen skiers who talk only about powder and stars. Around midnight, the sound of their skis awakens me. Their flight won't leave before tomorrow. They've decided to go to a hotel.

Outside, the snow is falling again. I go up to the windows, wonder if Vlad can see it from his hospital bed, whether, not being able to sleep, Luc is watching it, too. A group of young soldiers, their rifles slung across their chests, goes by. I wander off to T2C, sleep for a while on a seat, then behind a check-in counter, on a little bit of carpeting. Tomorrow, I'll have to get up before the first round of dog patrols. I should wash up, too.

FORT APACHE

The nickname given to Building 7200 which holds
the airport-maintenance services.

CHAPTER 31

It's after 10 a.m. The moving walkways are deserted this morning, I can't take them alone: Josias often hangs out around them, he would notice me instantly. The minutes go by. Finally, a group emerges. I blend into their mass, and go through the huge corridor 'without incident'. Neither Moumoune nor Thierry are in their usual places, and there's no sign of Trois in front of Door 3. Have they all been taken away?

Once or twice a year, Emmaüs offers a 'get-away' to those who live at the airport permanently, with the objective of helping them rediscover all the benefits of a 'normal' life. From what I've been told, the farm where they go is huge, and everything built of cut stone. Everyone gets up, eats and goes to bed at fixed times. Showers are obligatory, as are activities. Josias loves going there.

'On Wednesday, I do pottery, and the other days I take care of the cows.'

Ah, yes, the cows—he really loves them.

'There's something crazy in their eyes, and then all that white milk that comes out of their udders!'

Liam helps in the kitchens. The others, I don't remember. Impossible, in any case, to imagine Joséphine or Robocop in a natural setting, much less Trois, who hates going anywhere. In the bus that brings them back to the airport, some of them sometimes float the idea of returning 'to the surface'. Delighted, the guys from Emmaüs promise any takers fourteen thousand types of help. To no avail. As soon as they return to the airport, the memories of the smell of apples and good soup fade as fast as a dream. In less than twenty-four hours, it's as if none of them had ever left: no one washes, and they all begin to eat with their fingers again.

'Anna!'

That strength with which he hugs me.

'My God, I'm so happy to see you.'

He talks non-stop. Yesterday, he was so upset, he didn't know how to say goodbye to me. He felt so clumsy . . . I'm really happy to see him, too.

'Anna, force me to forget her, I can't bear what the pain is doing to me.'

Forget—he doesn't know what he's talking about! He's unaware, and I start laughing. He is so handsome . . . I look at him as a challenge.

'I have an idea, but you don't have to go along, OK?'

He's intrigued, but agrees. I take his hand.

'Are you ready?'

He nods his head again, without really understanding. It doesn't matter. I so need to show him who I really am.

I lead him towards the crowd of travellers. I tell the first people we encounter that we're a couple of cavers. To the next, that our little five-year-old girl has just had an operation. To the third, that we are executives and are joining our 'staff' for a retreat to 'reinforce connections'. The amazement in his eyes. The energy it gives me. I am unable to stop myself. We have two children; no, unfortunately, none. Our mother has just died. Our eldest son is getting married. He's a Buddhist. We've only just met. He's my brother-in-law, my brother, my younger brother, my twin. We're at the head of an association for the protection of fishing. We are veterinarians, literature professors, electricians, opera fans . . .

After the first lie, he begs me to stop, but gradually, listening to the enormities that I blurt out, seeing the empathy they provoke, his defences, in spite of himself, relax. He even starts to smile. Four children, yes, I hear him say, two of whom are studying in Shanghai. A breed farm with fifty dwarf Labradors, too. The guy is startled. 'Are there really dwarf Labradors?' 'A rare breed,' he responds. Furthermore, he is one of the only people to breed them in Europe. The man leaves, amazed. It takes all my strength to keep from laughing.

Mumbai, Djibouti, Porto, Tbilisi, Bristol, Erevan, San Francisco, Minneapolis, Cracow, Goteborg, Calgary, Mombasa, Verona, Canton, Nagoya, Toulouse, Tehran, Casablanca, Thessalonica, Alicante . . .

He gets the hang of it. Islamabad and Tehran, wonderful, the people, above all. A day didn't go by that we weren't invited somewhere! I laugh with him while looking around me from the corner of my eye. But there's no trace of Joséphine or Josias. Would Emmaüs really have taken them away in this awful weather? Unless they've all been evacuated to emergency centres. Unlike journalists who, in finding such a scoop, would descend like flies, we don't like those who die of the cold here.

THE PARIS AIRPORT
This is where the voyage begins

Towards the end of the day, he thanks me for this gift that was as unexpected as it was enjoyable. Never would he have believed that he could 'forget her that way'.

When he's about to leave, he can't help talking to me about her, again. The way she had of laughing right in the middle of their arguments, of never taking anything too seriously, their very intimate marriage, the gift she had given him: a piece of the wall in the garden of his childhood home (she had gone into the yard and stolen it, yes!), her passion for languages, mainly Italian, her talent as a gardener, the silence in which she would seek refuge, becoming inaccessible.

I listen to him without speaking. I see his lips tremble.

In front of the lift, he begs me. This fear he has, since he's met me, of being alone.

'Come to my house, Anna, let's spend the night together.'

His intimacy confounds me. How can I agree to leave the airport? This is where my entire life is. He looks at me sadly.

'Is it because of my wife?'

I wasn't even thinking of her. I lower my head and lie.

'Yes.'

'Then let's go to your place . . .'

How can I answer?

'My place is complicated . . . to a hotel, if you'd like. There are a lot here.'

But 'here', with the coming and going of aeroplanes, he'll spend the night thinking only of her, and *that* he doesn't want.

Behind him, the lift doors open.

He turns around and disappears again.

CHAPTER 32

I slept well last night. But will he be here? I'm so afraid I upset him by refusing to sleep at his place. I finally see him. He turns towards me. Handsome. So handsome, with that smile he gives me, one that conveys not the slightest reproach. He takes my face in his hands.

'You, too, lost someone you love in that plane . . .'

I stiffen.

'Sorry, Anna, forget what I just said.'

Forget. He definitely has only that verb in his mouth. I could almost laugh. But instead of that, I lead him into the terminals.

'Where are we going this morning, Luc? Norway, southern Italy?'

★

To draw outside oneself and inside oneself a circle, a second circle, a third. Erect solid, transparent walls all around. Sit at the centre of this splendid construction. No longer move. Then start dreaming. Only that. Dream. Dream of the body, the space of the body. Dream to the point of losing memory, erase every boundary. Even the gestures that speak of pain. Sit right

here. In the celestial whiteness of this kingdom. At the heart of its mute soft-
ness. Not to get heavier, not to fly away. Dream, just that, your chin on your
knees, become the time of the dream itself, its space, its language. Decide
never to leave it. Close oneself up for ever in the enchantment of that world.

★

This meeting every morning at 10 in front of the Arrivals doors, as if we had agreed on it, but not really, barely a murmured 'see you tomorrow'. This eagerness to meet them all, our imaginary, embroidered lives: luggage lost in Jakarta, baptism in Washington. Three Russians who, in turn, tell us about their stores in Moscow, a woman from Dublin, seventy-two years old, a glass of vodka in one gulp, *Long live Ireland!* An airline pilot transferred to Roissy in '69 . . .

'That year, I attended a boxing match organized by some Air France pilots, guess where? On the runways, can you imagine?! Inconceivable, eh? Back then, all this security mess didn't exist. The planes landed, we'd meet passengers at the bottom of the steps: stars, high-level people. Another world. Charters with Mister and Missus Everyone, we saw them coming around the middle of the Seventies. After the Vietnam War, the Yanks found themselves with so many bars on their hands! They sold them to some savvy folks who sensed the wind was turning; that was the beginning of mass tourism. Do you mind if I have another coffee?'

'Not at all, please.'

'As you've probably guessed, the world of flying and me, it was love at first sight. Still today, I must say. The language we have, all those codes. We're the only ones who understand them. If I tell you for example that my colleague is in the bathtub, you'll give me a funny look, right? I would guess you would! For us, the "bathtub" is a satellite box—and tourists are "swimsuits"!'

To forget—he is so right. The two of us, facing the world, of course I see that crowd. No, I don't know. He wants me to ask? Where did you say? From Mecca? Touch you, but why? It brings luck, really? Ten years of marriage, for us, yesterday, yes, yes, I assure you . . . but what . . .

'They're going to sing for you.'

'Sing?'

'For your anniversary, here, sit down.'

The men hand us their cushions, the women serve us tea. Who doesn't know about the return from the Hajj? Flight attendants go by, smiling. How many are you here waiting for the two pilgrims? Fifty? Sixty? Uncles, aunts, sisters, brothers, cousins. Some have travelled across France to meet them. And now the strident ululations of the women, their teeth, their laughter embracing us.

Such free-flowing days spent in his presence, how many hours, how many days? This force, every afternoon, that pushes us outside: Spot Site #12, south-facing; Spot Site #15, south-facing; Spot Site #7, north-facing; the freezing wind on our hands. Guards who don't arrest us, who even greet us.

'No, today, take that road that goes to the right.'

'But Anna . . . the runways, they're on the other side.'

'They are so majestic, Luc, I want you to see them.'

'Who, Anna?'

Going through the freight zones, horns honking, tunnel.

'The two cedars over there, can you see them?'

We get out of the car and begin walking towards them.

'They're over two hundred years old, did you know that?'

But how could he know? When we get to them, I ask him to lie down under their branches. He looks at me, not understanding. Is this 'visit' part of the 'game', too? I gesture to him not to speak, to close his eyes. Six men with their arms stretched out couldn't reach around their trunks.

'Anna . . .'

'Please, Luc, listen.'

Not the outside world, no, the branches, the movement of the branches, the folds they make in the sky, two hundred years, does he realize, it was a botanist who brought them here from England, back in the day, there were only fields here, scarcely a few humans. He turns towards me, stupefied, asks me where I learnt all that. I tell him, evasive, that I read it somewhere. And many other things. Legend has it that Pompidou had flown over the area in a helicopter, and demanded that they save the cedars, not the houses, no, not the farms, but these two cedars absolutely, even if it were to cause problems, and that's why they've survived . . .

'Unlike all the rest.'

A Thai Airlines Airbus 310 that is rising above us, the smell of resin, of sap. What if we decided to live here, Luc? Protected for ever, close to God.

'Because they come from God, you know? All trees come from God.'

He looks at me.

'Tell me about yourself, Anna. I still know nothing about you.'

But it's so lovely today, and we're so happy.

AIR FRANCE
Make the sky the most beautiful place on earth

When night falls, his invariable question:

'May I take you home?'

My invariable response:

'No, Luc.'

Day after day, evening after evening, his frustration, his growing confusion.

'Are you sure?'

'Yes, Luc.'

Our two bodies separate, he goes to the edge of the airport, increasingly perplexed, I, once he has disappeared, into the airport, being very careful not to be noticed, so careful that some nights I don't sleep, just doze in restrooms, underneath the parking lots, in the service hangars . . .

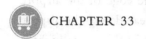 CHAPTER 33

Nights that go on for ever and whose end I await evermore urgently, so eager am I to see him. Everywhere else, it's as if the world has stopped. No sign of Joséphine, Josias or Vlad, not even Lucien, whose cafe has had a 'closed' sign in the window for more than two weeks.

Aeromexico Boeing 772, Delta 'Habitat for Humanity' Boeing 763, Cimber Air Boeing 737, Pakistan Airbus 310.

'Excuse me, but it is strictly forbidden to take photos.'

'We're not taking photos.'

'You can't stay here.'

We pretend to leave, go back the way we came, run into a Canadian fellow holding a camera who is shooting in every direction.

'Excuse us, could you take our photo in front of the A320?'

'Are you spotters?'

'Sometimes, yes.'

'I do this every weekend. Yesterday, I saw a CityJet Fokker 50. I didn't know they had bought them. Here, look at all the ones I saw yesterday, not bad, eh? Hey, have you seen an Air Canada Vancouver 777 with a crazy design? I got a blurry shot of it last week, and can't find it again.'

'Sorry, no.'

'If you see it, here, I'll give you my number.'

'We'll contact you, promise.'

'A tip: the most beautiful spot in the airport is the roof of the Sheraton, slip Victorine 20 euros, but shhh, you didn't hear it from me! Take it easy!'

 CHAPTER 34

The roof of the Sheraton. Top of the world.

'Luc, isn't it magnificent?'

No, he doesn't care for it. But it's so crazy to be up here.

'Watch out! Vrroooommmm, I'm an aeroplane!'

'Anna . . .'

'Propulsion! Jetwash! Wing, tip of the wing, get in Luc, go up with me!'

He's not even smiling. Too bad, I'm flying off. Expulsion! Gas! The two of us, Luc, heart everywhere, sky, damn, it's beautiful, arms, wind, hands, cities above your head, low-flying zzzzzzzzz, did you see how the earth is unfolding? That's it, wahooooooo, my wings are changing direction! I'm spinning, Luc! The clouds are inverted! Heads turning the world, vrrrrrreeee!'

'Anna, please . . .'

Our bodies are so vast! The sky everywhere to the ends of the earth.

'Anna . . .'

'Do you see how I'm gliding!'

Whiteness of my body, clouds in one mouthful.

'Anna, stop now!'

But I'm drunk, too many emotions.

'Portholes! Wingtips! Vortices!'

'Anna!'

This darkness in me, this sudden explosion of unleashed night, careful zooooooom, I'm flying! Fragmented speed, good God but why am I swerving! Mass time that falls, rain, the din of rain, little girl! Such a clean house, tree, Luc! Trunks everywhere sky!

'Anna!!!'

That voice . . . I open my eyes.

'Let go of me, Luc, you're hurting me.'

He looks at me, he's frightened.

'Anna, my God, you almost jumped!!'

Such sorrow in me.

'Anna, this can't go on. Come on, let's go down. You have to talk to me.'

In the car, his hands are trembling on the steering wheel. As if he didn't have enough with one dead woman in his life! Do I realize? I turn away without a word, stare at the thick snowflakes settling on the windshield. He's right: What got hold of me? He grabs my arm, forces me to look at him.

'Anna, talk to me or . . .'

I let out a nervous laugh.

'Or what, Luc?'

I am a hole that shelters destruction. When is he going to understand that? Inside me, aeroplanes shatter, bodies fall into wells, husbands pace like lions in a cage, women scream in silence, cars fly

. . . But he's beside himself. If he hadn't been there . . . the words get caught in his throat.

'Anna, I want us to stop now.'

I give him an icy stare. In the end, he's no better than one of those customs and immigration cops who pride themselves on expulsing women and children.

'OK, you asked for it. My head is empty, Luc.'

'What do you mean, empty?'

I point at my head.

'Empty, nothing, nada!'

'Anna, what are you saying?'

That black anger rising in me.

'I can't even remember my name. Anna, it's the best I could come up with.'

He stares at me, dumbfounded.

'You mean . . . your name isn't . . . Anna?'

'One chance in a million.'

'But . . . your husband? The crash?'

'Same.'

'You . . . you made everything up?'

'In a way.'

The confusion in his eyes.

'But then . . . why the airport? Why the Rio flight?'

'You would never have believed me otherwise.'

He turns his head away, incapable of saying another word.

'Now please let's go, Luc, take me back to the airport.'

He doesn't move, and I'm suddenly really angry at him. He should never have forced me to tell him that. Weren't we the rulers of the world in that airport? Why not continue the game to the end? It's as if we had to return to disaster.

'Start the car now.'

But nothing, no reaction from him. So I open the door and get out of the car.

'Anna!'

Why can't I be a stone? Something that doesn't speak, that doesn't feel, but that doesn't crumble? He takes my arm.

'Anna, come on, I'll take you back.'

I laugh meanly.

'Ah yes, but where will you take me, Luc?'

He looks at me, increasingly disconcerted.

'Well . . . home.'

Nothing, he has never really seen anything of me, or me only as the echo of his pain. I look at him, disgusted.

'Don't you understand that that is where I sleep?!'

The stupor in his eyes.

'Give me my suitcase now.'

He still doesn't move and, standing in the snow, my anger dissipates. In my past, how many dead would he guess there have been? Husband and daughters up in smoke. As if it were easy to carry that around, as if it were something I wanted to shout off the rooftops.

'I've been living in the airport for more than eight months. Before, I don't know. A big house with a man I didn't love any more and a fridge full of vegetables. It seems crazy to you, right? It's much worse, Luc. In my dreams, two little girls are playing hide-and-seek. The smallest one falls into a well. The others, I don't know. I'm driving on a straight road and . . .'

'And what, Anna?'

But it's too late.

'Nothing. Drop me off now.'

'No, Anna, not after what you've just told me.'

He looks around helplessly.

'But, where would I drop you off?'

I point to the airport.

'Home.'

He shakes his head.

'My home, that is.'

Clearly, he hasn't understood.

'Do you see the fence over there? When I got here, I swore to myself that I would never pass through it, or I'd lose everything again, and that's not going to happen.'

'Anna, you can't really spend the rest of your life here.'

'Oh yes, I can.'

He looks at me, frightened, starts the car without another word.

On my right, after we pass a bridge, a rabbit leaps out of the snow. When it sees me, it freezes. That despair in the depths of its eyes. Luc accelerates slowly and the rabbit runs off. Under the white sky, it is soon only a dark shadow.

'I'll take you to a hotel.'

The pity in his voice, as if he were talking to a poor madwoman.

'No, Luc.'

'I'll pay.'

'Out of the question.'

He brakes and stops the car. The day after we met, he could have not shown up and ended up killing himself, but he came back and waited for me in front of Arrivals. All these days, he could have also lied to me, as I did to him. He really believed it, my story of a dead husband in that fucking plane. Finally, someone who had gone through the same nightmare. He's overwhelmed by the feeling of having been had.

'Take the room, Anna.'

I don't dare refuse him. He continues to drive in silence.

In front of the Ibis Hotel, he gets out of the car and asks me to bring my suitcase and join him at Reception . On the other side of the glass doors, I see him holding out his credit card. When I appear, the woman gives me a big smile. With a nervous gesture, he hands me the key.

'I've paid for three nights.'

He turns to leave without even saying goodbye. From the lobby I watch him disappear into his car. This time, I'm sure, he will not return.

CHAPTER 35

Lying on the bed, I turn on the TV, I turn it off, I turn it on, I zap, I stop for a few seconds on the spectacle of thousands of pink flamingos flying over a river in Africa. Vlad never asked me about my past. With him, I wasn't threatened. The dream, at his side, endured, and that was all that mattered. With Luc, it's exactly the opposite, and yet, it is he, this evening, whom I miss. I stifle a nervous laugh. As if, after all I said to him, I still had a chance of seeing him. He might have excused my lying, but being crazy *and* homeless? And why did he try to stop me from jumping off the roof of the Sheraton? The more he told me to stop, the more I needed to escape him, as if he were forcing me to face the woman I was so afraid of finding again. There is something so wounded in her. So desperate. Why, Luc, why force me to experience that night again?

But you are already so far away. I even wonder if I invented you, too.

I keep getting up, try to open the window, rinse my face. Just before dawn, I suddenly fall asleep. The shock of the branches, the cracking of the twigs. I run, barefoot, through the forest, a horde on my heels. It's gaining on me. I run faster without noticing the thorns tearing at my skin. They are now upon me. Terrified, I turn my head:

there's light up ahead! Full of hope, I push on without seeing the tree that is standing in front of me and which I run into at full speed.

Indeed, reintegrating yourself is what we're talking about. You don't understand, there are no benefits for people like you. Two job losses in such a short time, which in addition proves to me that you are truly handicapped? You're not the only one in that case, madame. What can I do if there are roaches? No, there's no more room for you this evening. Come back tomorrow. Yes, tomorrow. If your family doesn't want to put you up, there must be a reason, right? A good reason. What? You don't need to be reintegrated? No, not fired, we just don't need your services any more. It's 1,200 euros per month and, if you're not happy, there's a long waiting list. You're sleeping on the street? The campers are all taken. Of course your husband has an obligation, but we don't know where he is, and anyway, your house has been sold. Showers, and then what? What's that, memory problems? Where are you sleeping? Because we're telling you we can't take you in any more! I'm not Abbot Peter, after all! Don't worry, we'll find something, madame. You only have 3 euros? Showers are once a week. What can I do if they're violent? There are houses for mental patients! Hang tight, come back tomorrow. If you think you're the first to be ripped off in their fucking emergency centres, thank God you weren't beaten up. You don't qualify, no. The doctors' opinions vary. I can call, but they're not answering. Are you sure he still lives in France? Don't stress about it. Your brain just needs to rest. This file isn't complete. Yesterday, you remember, but not today? But who are you exactly? Who?

I wake up, my teeth chattering, and curl up under the covers. Did all of that really happen? But where? When? And why wasn't Marc there? Was it before the accident? After? I burrow deeper.

Outside, the sun is coming up.

CHAPTER 36

In the empty restaurant, I wait for Barbara to walk away from the buffet before I stuff a plastic bag with rolls, little jars of jam and chocolate croissants. I might as well take as much as possible before I leave the hotel for good. But, just as I'm taking a few more rolls, a hand rests softly on mine. I turn around, ready to argue: Where is it written that one must eat breakfast in the restaurant, and what about busy guests like me? But it's he, it's Luc. I look at him, amazed. That violent desire, and that fear, as well, which drowns me. He's about to take me in his arms, but I gently push him away.

'Do you want me to leave?'

I was already so far away.

'It was really difficult without you these past few days . . . I thought . . .'

I gesture for him not to say anything more. This pain that over-whelms everything. I can't bear it any more.

'Let me help you, Anna.'

Everything is destroyed. What can he do for me?

'I'm like you, Anna, I don't know anything. Let's just rest a bit then walk, talk . . . We'll see.'

We're lying on the bed, he hugs me very gently. Soon our tongues touch. Glued against him, I open up, but, once again, he suddenly freezes. On the verge of tears, he rolls over onto the other side of the bed. That pain, where she's left him. Some days, he even hates her. Couldn't she have taken a different flight? Why did she do that to him? I close my eyes, rest my head on his lap.

'Tell me about you, Anna, tell me about your life in the airport.'

'Right now?'

'Yes, right now. The places where you slept. The people you met. Everything, Anna.'

But how can I unveil that world without betraying them all? There's the story of the Cuban woman apprehended by two cops from Customs and Immigration as soon as she arrived.

'*Madre di Dios, mi amigo mi espera a su casa, tengo la su attestacion, que pasa?*'

'Calm down, madame.'

In front of the bewildered crowd, she shouted even louder, swore she was legal. Nothing worked. Ten minutes later, when most of the onlookers had already forgotten, she was asked to go into the restroom and pee into a jar. Woe was she if she refused, because the cops were going to take her right away to the X-Ray room where Carlion, the airport doctor (whose great-grandfather was also a doctor, in Cayenne), would have her stand in front of his X-ray machine and 'scan' her insides. After which, they would have waited a few minutes while the Customs officers bemoaned the fact that dealers, today, preferred to move merchandise on the roads rather than by planes because of the increasingly sophisticated security controls. Then Carlion would have come out of his dark little room and not been able to resist telling the Cuban woman why he had X-rayed her like that. Twenty years earlier, a young woman wasn't feeling

well, and had been brought to him. Her symptoms said it all: barbi-
turate overdose. But pumping her stomach didn't reveal anything, and
the young woman died. Nothing? Impossible! Carlion demanded an
autopsy which proved him right . . . with a twist. Ensuring her fatal
end, she had stuck those barbiturates up her anus! Since then, he
always gave a rectal exam to any comatose patient brought to him. In
1981, he had an odd heroin overdose case: not one needle mark on
the guy's body! Two fingers in his anus, and there it was! A ball of
wax full of white powder! That was how he discovered his first
'baller', and it wouldn't be his last. These days, travellers ingested
capsules, at least 30, and sometimes as many as a hundred.

'What about you, dear, *cuantas*?' he would have asked.

The young Cuban woman would have shaken her head. She
didn't have anything. Nada. Then, Carlion would have gone to get
the X-rays which he would have put right under her nose and
under those of the Customs officers. After observing for a minute,
in an almost religious silence, he would have either had her released,
or, pointing out here and there a bunch of capsules filled with
heroin or other dubious substances (or worse, explosives), he would
have gestured to the officers, finally the lucky winners, to take her
away.

Luc looks at me. He's stupefied. What does that story have to
do with me? I look away. Her great fear of being discovered, her
physical resistance, is just like mine. But he shakes his head. What
he wants to hear are names of people, places. My story seems so
impossible to him.

So impossible.

So, to appease him, I start telling him about Titi and Moumoune
who have been living as a couple there for seventeen years. About
Albert who is regularly found naked in the restroom in T2E. About

Geronimo who shouts at night in the corridors, about Paulette, lying down day and night next to the moving walkway in T2F, about Georges who always brandishes his rosary, about them all, staff and travellers, who every day fill and vacate the places I've been wandering through for more than seven months. I don't tell him about Vlad, his brutal way of penetrating me, his illness, our incinerated things, about the crazy love Josias feels for me, his brother Liam's notebook, Joséphine's hatred. I tell him that for all those months I've slept on seats or while hiding in sub-level rooms discovered by chance, taking food from trash bins or from tables . . .

'There you have it.'

I haven't told him everything, and he knows it. It doesn't matter. He can better imagine me now. Coming and going, listening to the world.

Unnoticeable.

And now? I ask him if he wants to go back and see the planes.

'No, Anna. I want to be with you, just be with you.'

But then where, Luc? He answers that we could take the VAL. Walk. This time, I'm the one who refuses. Who knows if Joséphine and Josias have returned? Back there they might find me.

'Let's take the car, instead.'

★

How many days has he been going through windows to come and sit beside her? Everyone would really like to know through which ruse he has managed to join her, how he met her, too, and why, when he leaves, she remains seated, not moving, instead of following him. Is it they who frighten her? They who would so like to meet her.

Day after day, however, she refuses, leaving them every evening, a bit more alone, more naked, too. Fortunately, the next day, he reappears, and it is as if he were digging something in her. Something on the order of an out-pouring that she increasingly has trouble containing. One can see impercep-tible signs of this: the slight weakening of her shoulders, the trembling of her fingers, the relaxation of her neck. Henceforth, everyone holds their breath. There is such calm there. Inside themselves, they would like to eat something, kneel down, hold out their arms. But she shakes her head. There is such sadness in her.

One day, however, it's as if the windows had disappeared and, for the first time, they hear what she says to him. But since I tell you that I'm floating here. But because I tell you that here there is no history. But because I tell you that here tears have no weight. But because I tell you that here I am the other. But because I tell you that here I don't suffer. But because I tell you that here I can't die, because only bodies die. And what is the body? Where is the body? When and where does it begin? Is there still a body when there is no more memory?

Outside, the snow has stopped falling. It's spring. How many years has he come to visit her, maybe centuries, because everywhere else there are still wars and pitiful cries. Seated, from the back, one can guess she's on the verge of tears. The children's balls hit against the windows. Will he come this day when she will finally decide to get up?

But because I tell you that here I am the other. But because I tell you that here I don't suffer. But because I tell you that here I can't die, because only bodies die. And what is the body? Where is the body? When and where does it begin? Is there still a body when there is no more memory?

CHAPTER 37

Days driving around in his car. Out of a tacit understanding, and as if to push the desire we feel as far away as possible, we engage in endless conversation. He tells me about his childhood spent in a big house in the country, about how fascinated he was with the force of water, about the profession that very quickly attracted him. Hydraulic engineer, specialist in the treatment of wastewater. Six months earlier, he asked for a year's sabbatical. As for me, I tell him about the anguish of the first days, the encounters with some travellers, with Liam, Josias, Lucien and Vlad, whom I describe as vaguely as I can, but whose names I want him to know, my 'washing up' in the restroom of T2F, my walks to the Concorde. I learn that he has two sisters, one is a professor in Montpellier, the other a wife and mother near Bordeaux. And I learn about his friends, their phone calls which he doesn't have the strength to answer.

Every evening, when we're about to part, I want to cling to him, beg him to stay. Instead, I turn away without a word. Sometimes, his presence makes me feel so bad that I tell him it's over. On those days, I pick up my suitcase and walk through the terminals trying again to become the traveller from before. But something is missing.

Something so painful that, back in the hotel room, I sit on the ground and rock back and forth for hours. Then a voice says: go back to him, leave here, go. A very soft voice that makes me even sadder. Believing that the car continues to draw circles in the air and that my screaming continues. Did I ever really get out of that pile of metal?

Outside the window, day is breaking. Lying on the bed, I stare at the ceiling. I felt so good back there. Why did you come, Luc, and why, the more I desire you, does everything in me unravel more? I probably will have to erase you, too. Except, even back there, it's not the same any more, it's as if having gotten closer to you has put the magic elsewhere, into a place that I don't know, that I can't find. So I decide to close my eyes until you return. Because you will return, it can't be otherwise, you are opening the door to the room. Anna, what's going on. Nothing, Luc, touch me, rock me, take that woman lost in pain away from me. You look at me sadly. Everything would be so simple outside this airport. Here, the memory of your wife reigns so powerfully, everything reminds you of her last look. I stand up, I rebel. The little I have left, it is in fact here that I've found it. Is that what he wants to make me lose?

'No, Anna.'

'If I leave here, that's what will happen.'

'No, Anna.'

Weary, he starts the car again, starts driving in increasingly more anarchic circles. One afternoon, he suggests we stop in Aéroville, to buy me a sweater and watch a film. I shrug my shoulders, there are too many 'normal' people there, not enough travelling, not enough suitcases . . . Finally it's night. He asks if I want to return to the hotel. I say I don't. A half-hour later he asks the same question. But no, just the idea of returning to that empty room again, of turning on

164

the light, illuminating that bed where he isn't waiting for me, no. He looks at me without understanding.

'Then where, Anna?'

'Somewhere . . . where we'll be alone, far from the city, and where we can hug each other.'

He asks if I'm sure. Of course not, I'm not sure. I'm so afraid of losing everything, but how can I imagine one more night without him, in that room? So, not looking at me, he sets off. That fear that rises in me and which I try to overcome: sentences, words, thoughts that are all mixed up and form a wave that crests on itself. Where is it here? Under its furious roiling, the terminals explode. Hold on, leave as quickly as possible, swim among the debris, warn Josias, Vlad, get to the surface, but it's the entire airport that the wild waters are carrying away, bodies that I bump into, bodies on my face, such a hard woman, so implacable, hold on, don't turn around, laughing little girls on the edges of wells, where then, is their laughter, Luc, their such soft voices in the light of the sky? Will the wave carry them off, too, and the aeroplanes that saved me?

'Luc, no, go back.'

He's kissing my neck.

'We're here, Anna.'

Such silence around us. I slowly raise my head. The airport is so far away and I've forgotten nothing. I almost feel like laughing, sobbing all of a sudden. Come on, he murmurs. Come on? But where? I so want to hug him to me.

'Me, too, Anna, but under the trees, over there.'

Our footsteps sink into the earth and very soon so do our bodies. It's been so long. No frenzy or impatience. Just him and me, undressing very slowly under this vault of leaves. He spreads his coat on the ground, we lie down next to each other. With infinite patience, he caresses me without taking his eyes off me. The skin of our hands brushing, touching. I tremble from this love that is finally released. He takes off his sweater, then mine, then my shirt. Here I am, naked in front of him, and he enters me. Oh, that eye, his, that never leaves me and where I so powerfully offer myself up. Cries scarcely murmured, so vast inside, however, and with each movement I sound out beyond that night of trees and leaves. My fingers cling to his face, his fingers. How long do we stay like that so intensely climaxing, scarcely audible, in the immensity?

Until then, the world had no origin. Now it has one, in which Liam, Joséphine, Vlad, Lucien, Josias, luminous, are dancing. Oh, their laughter that makes me so light. Nothing will ever be erased again. Luc is there from now on. He takes my hand, pulls me up. That evening, we can sleep at his place if I want. No, not yet, but tomorrow or the day after, yes, I promise.

So he takes me back, but, this time, comes with me into the room where, exhausted, we slip under the covers. He falls asleep very quickly. I look at him, happy. What words are there to express this incredible hope that is filling me? What words while I drift off in turn and while the cry of the seeker is filling the room.

When I open my eyes, I'm in a white room, surrounded by tall grass. What am I doing here? Slowly, I get up trying to remember how I got there. People whose faces I'm unable to see ask me questions that I don't understand. I try to find out who they are, but the very last image I remember is the one where I see myself singing behind the wheel of a car while the seeker, in the distance, is counting. The hours go by. I'm cold. Outside, unless it's inside my head, I hear people calling: Élodie! Élodie! Then, that shout. A terrible shout that makes me tremble so violently that everything suddenly comes back. She, over there, balancing on the edge of the well! Come, come, I found something! My fear for her, her laughter, my crazy running, finally my hand,

MY HAND turning the wheel and pushing her! The thump of the little body at the bottom of the well. THUMP! while the car spins in the air and, in the rear-view mirror, just before hitting the tree, the spectacular white of the tree, I see her little face for the last time . . .

'Anna? Anna, are you still asleep?'

Élodie, my little sister, my little girl!

He shakes me gently.

'Anna, are you awake?'

From under the covers, I ask him to go wait for me in the breakfast room and to order me a coffee. He closes the door softly, saying 'see you in a minute!' Under the covers, I am petrified. My hands, if he knew. In the corridor, I hear his footsteps moving away. Stricken, I get up. I leave.

 CHAPTER 38

The VAL platform. Three Japanese women in kilts. Head lowered, I enter the first carriage. What sort of creature pushes her little sister down a well and kills her own child? Stop at Terminal 2. I lock myself in one of the closest toilet stalls. Here, it's certain, he won't be able to find me. The hours go by.

'Could you come out, please? There's no more toilet paper any-where, and I really need to go.'

The woman starts knocking on the door.

'Are you deaf or what?'

I open the door, she bumps into me.

'It's about time!'

Find another place, quickly, I'm so afraid of running into him. And all these travellers who are staring at me.

'Are you looking for me?'

I almost faint when I see him.

'Vlad???'

'Did you really think I was dead?'

The extreme harshness of his voice. He notices my new suitcase, and barks a mean laugh.

'At least my money was used for something.'

I look at him, stunned. The destruction of the camp, his books, everything burnt, does he really think I could have . . .

'Cat got your tongue?'

'No, Vlad, it's just that I didn't do anything . . . the camp, it was the Russians who . . .'

'That's it, the Russians!'

'Vlad, I swear . . .'

He turns away.

'Don't say anything else.'

It's only at that moment that I realize he's there, visible to everyone, that he wasn't arrested after all. I catch up to him, full of questions.

'Vlad . . . they gave you your papers? All is good?'

He looks at me harshly.

'There's no more Vlad. Go on, get lost or you'll be sorry.'

Around us, passengers are leaving for Brisbane, Kursk. I bite my lip until it bleeds. Vlad doesn't move a muscle. So I turn around and I run, I run, I run, I run, praying that my memory will blow apart for the second time, annihilating everything.

Annihilating everything.

Lost in the immensity. Travellers knocking into me. Red badges knocking into me. Doors, shouts from the people which, every second, hit me more violently. Why did I have to remember? Here, without a memory, the world finally entered me. I drank it up. And I loved again. Why?

 CHAPTER 39

Nights without sleeping, days without eating. Knees folded under my chin, I sleep an hour or two, here, in the restroom, over there, against the wall of a service room.

One night, my heart stopped beating when I saw the note written in black ink on the mirror of the T2F restroom: 'Anna, I'm looking for you everywhere, I beg you, call me, 06-19-78-19-64, Luc.' To hear his voice. The temptation is strong. But how can I look him in the eyes when, in my head, there is their joyful laughter before I . . . No, he must forget me. I never existed.

The days go by. I don't wash any more, I don't comb my hair any more. Ten times I come across Vlad, ten times I beg him to listen to me. I have something so important to tell him, something only he can hear. Each time, he pushes me away.

'Get lost, I'm telling you!'

'Is it because of the camp? You still think I did it?'

'Leave.'

'What is it then? Is it because you told me about your wife and children?' His face abruptly changes expression.

'How . . .'

'You talked about them when you had a fever. You even asked me to get their photo.'

Pale, he turns away.

'You don't know what you're talking about.'

'Vlad, turn around, talk to me, I beg you.'

But he starts shouting.

'Go away!'

I abandon my suitcase, watch from a distance, apathetic, the anti-bomb people working around it, the dull sound it makes when they destroy it.

'*Little Joachim is waiting for his parents in front of Door 30.*'

'Are you waiting for a plane to arrive?'

He's wearing the uniform of a security guard. I let out a 'no', stand up under his wary look, and walk to the exit. Outside, the wind is glacial. Travellers jump into taxis, others run, their suitcases in hand. My fingers are soon so frozen that I can't move them any more.

'Are you waiting for someone?'

It's two cops and they're watching me suspiciously. I turn around, go back into the hall. Three travellers are talking about an air pocket they hit because of that terrible storm above Nairobi, which scared them to death. I turn my head, stare at the lifts for a long time before entering one. Let at least one person know before I'm forced to leave.

In the underground parking lot, behind the eleven carts that encircle them, the three of them are snoring: people here who endure and before whom, cowering in the shadows, I can feel I'm fainting.

'Shit, how many days has it been since you've eaten? Here, take a bite of this sandwich.'

He can't believe he's seeing me. He pats my cheeks.

'Your Vlad, I begged him to tell me where you were. Me and Liam looked all over for you, you know. Everywhere! Come on, eat some more.'

'Josias . . .'

'Shh, it's over now, stop crying. Your Josias is here, we don't give a shit about the rest.'

 CHAPTER 40

Going through Terminals A-B-C. Going down the service stairs in T2C to Level -1 up to a door 'area off-limits to the public' that in less than two minutes, with the help of an old hanger, Josias unlocks. A corridor down which he makes me run. Another door, this time unlocked, that opens onto a passage that ends with a little winding staircase that climbs up endlessly. A climb that seems to last an eternity and which makes me dizzy. I hang on to the railing to catch my breath. Where are we going?

'You wanted a camp, yes or no? We're almost there, hang on.'

He turns around, then disappears above. When I reach the last step, what I see is so unexpected that I let out a small cry of surprise. At my feet, the entire air-filtration system of the airport extends for what seems forever.

'So was it worth it?'

'Yes, Josias, but . . .'

'Wait, you haven't seen everything!'

He points at the ceiling to an open trap door.

'You're not serious.'

'Don't worry, you get up on my back and . . .'

'Josias, I'm exhausted, I'm not going up there.'

'Don't be a pain in the arse, wrap your legs around me and pull yourself up by leaning on either side, there, like that.'

In a final effort, I manage to get my shoulders, arms, and soon my entire body through the door. Below, Josias is shouting.

'So, was I right to make you do it?'

The space unfolds over more than two hundred meters, enclosed by a window that reveals the entire airport. No walls, no furniture. A naked vista expanding to infinity. I stand there, my mouth gaping, opposite my gigantic shadow on the ground that is catapulted by beams of light from projectors which, from the buildings across the way, sweep the world, bathing me every ten seconds in their glow. I help pull him up, and Josias joins me.

'You can sleep easy here. This is the airport attic. No one will bother you here. You can access the other side, too, but all the machines are there and the noise is terrible. Here, there's nothing at all! Beautiful, isn't it?'

'Yes.'

'With the snow, it was even better, where were you all those days?'

'. . .'

'Will you tell me?'

'Yes, I'll tell you.'

'Good, I'm going, I don't want the mother to freak out, do you want me to bring you some water?'

'No, I'm OK.'

'Don't leave without telling me, OK? It was really sad without you here.'

He leaves me alone looking out the window: comings and goings on the tarmac, FedEx, Airlinair trucks, loading of mail sacks, cleaning crews. I close my eyes. Let my tears flow. It should be me, a prisoner in a car, at the bottom of a well. It should be me.

Dead.

Nowhere else.

 CHAPTER 41

'Hey, it's me . . .'

I stare for a moment at the man opposite me without recognizing him, then quickly stand up.

'Josias?!'

He has shaved his beard, cut his hair, put on impeccably clean clothes.

'Look at the ladder I found for you! I brought a mattress, too. Super good quality that I got from the guys on the site of the International Trade Centre they're constructing . . .'

He lies down next to me, looks at me.

'So will you kiss me now?'

'Josias, I've killed.'

He rolls his eyes.

'You, you've killed?'

'When I was a child, I pushed my sister down a well and, later, I killed my daughter.'

'But . . . why would you do such things?'

'I don't know.'

'Shit, you'll say anything!'

'I swear, Josias.'

He looks at me, suddenly serious.

'People who kill don't have skin like that.'

'Josias, you have to believe me, it's important.'

'Anyway, we can't do anything for the dead, and we're alive.'

'I killed them, Josias.'

'Can you see how I'm devouring you with my eyes?'

'Josias . . .'

'Kiss me.'

'No.'

But he doesn't stop. He's been waiting for this moment for a very long time. It's obviously not a story about little girls supposedly dead because of me that's going to dissuade him. He clings to me, tries to kiss me. I struggle to push him away.

'Shit, I'm clean, what more do you want?'

'I can't, with you, that's all.'

'That's all? I spent nights looking for you! But no, you have to get it from your Vlad, still and always, when I'm the one who saved him! Me!'

'Josias . . .'

He takes an envelope out of his pocket, hands it to me, shaking.

'Carlion found it on him. He didn't know who you were, I told him that I knew.'

'What . . .'

'I had sworn to myself I would never tell you. They found him yesterday, hanging, in one of the service corridors.'

'What do you mean, hanging . . .'

'Read his letter, you'll see, just never look for me again. Never!'

He turns away. I stay standing, not moving, my eyes staring at the envelope he gave me. On the front, in Vlad's lovely handwriting: 'For her.'

Dear you,

When you read these words, I will be gone. Don't ask me why I made this decision, it has been ripening in me for years, and now I am finally able to pass to the act. But, before, I want to tell you what no one knows, not even Carlion, who will read this letter, knowing however, that it is addressed only to you, how can I be mad at him?

P., the city where I lived, was nice. My wife and I were Serbs, our neighbours Croatians. At the school where I taught, I was truly bored. The students for the most part were mediocre. I had only one happiness in my life then: go back to my family every evening, hug them. One day, during the war, I found all three of them brutally assassinated in our house. But I'm not writing you this letter so you'll take pity on my fate. Far from it. I, too, caused blood to flow. And don't think that it was one of those moments of insanity when, after having experienced horror, one becomes a monster, too. No. It happened a year before my family was slaughtered, during the summer of '91. In the month of June that year, the head of my school suggested I join the Serbian forces during the summer holidays. He had connections, he could help. I was so bored, as I said. The year hadn't been good, the students worse than mediocre. As for my wife, he wrote a letter to her saying he was sending me for a month of training. Inspired both by a sense of patriotism and the desire to finally live something great, I agreed. Twenty days later, I participated in an offensive. The targeted village had two hundred inhabitants. In every house there were only terrified women and children. We pushed them outside. We gathered them in the courtyards. I was afraid. I was also very excited. The women were crying. A guy next to me slapped one of them, and I did the same. Shortly afterwards, two guys put a bullet in the head of another because she was shouting 'too loud'. The children were trembling. The mothers hugged them with all their strength. I have no excuse. I was fully aware. I just couldn't stop myself. I grabbed her by the hair. I dragged her into one of the rooms of the house. She fought. She screamed. I don't know how many hours I tortured her. I tied her down. I burnt her with my cigarettes, I cut her skin with a knife. The others did the same. In other rooms. The winner was the one who made his victim scream the loudest. I don't know how long it lasted. She spat out blood, and convulsed. I fled. Afterwards, I just walked, walked until the month was over, and I could go home. There, I lied to my wife, who asked me to tell her about the 'training'. It was good, I told her. Then, I went back to work. Normal life. A year later, I reassured my wife, panicked at the idea that I was going to be away a few days to visit my parents. The Croatians, I had seen them at work. So disorganized! They could never take the city. Leaving her there, I left with a light heart. Light! The rest you know. No, not yet everything. That nausea that has never left me, that disgust for my person. A final thing. You, when I saw you for the first time, the same face as hers. I should have fled from you. I watched you, discovering more each day, a little more, how beautiful you were, how much I had destroyed. The very beautiful life that we could have had together. But there is no redemption for men like me. None. And I had no right to hold you back the way I was doing. You deserve much better.

Vlad

PS. Don't forget to practice your English.

Outside the window, the sky is raging. I go down the tall ladder, then descend the steps of the small winding staircase. Once I'm down, I don't even try to run in the corridors to avoid the cameras. What difference does it make now? Leave this world, be done with it for good. Isn't that the meaning of his letter? Death is the only recourse for people like him and me. A group of pilots walk by on my right. Children playing ball. Mother shouting at them to stop.

'*Could you please . . .*'

Please what? I don't even answer. Vlad is gone.

He was so determined to make me keep my head up. But I'm the one who destroys everything, you know, Josias, who never again, because of me . . .

'*. . . could you please . . .*'

You, Vlad, whom I could have, and you, Luc. So much.

'. . . it's not possible . . .'

Because, no, there truly is nothing left. Everything has come unglued, the great scenery, the world introduced by that scenery . . . but when all of that is gone? I mean, me, Luc? What remains of my presence in the place where everyone in a single and same voice:

'*. . . Is it really true?*'

True what? The guy backs up, staring blankly. Fucking airport, where I couldn't keep anything, not even our love, Luc, the body of my little sister and my little girl. Clack! My steps are now advancing *no more*, while everyone, eyes, mouths, the entire hall in a single massive body is pointing at me.

'It's not possible . . .'

Only one more metre to cover, there it is, I reach the door, only one traveller emerges, mad with rage.

'There must be a way, it's not possible! Where are you going?'

'I'm going, leave me alone.'

'What do you mean, you're going?! No one can leave . . .'

'Leave me alone, I said I'm going.'

'What about me! I'll lose my job if I can't go!'

I take a step back, look for some help. No guard in sight.

'If you want to take a flight, you just need to consult the . . .'

But the departure board stuns me—I can't finish my sentence.

LONDON	AF 1450	CANCELLED
STRASBOURG	AF 4900	CANCELLED
BEIJING	UX 1006	CANCELLED
HELSINKI	LG 8012	CANCELLED
MOSCOW	AF1722	CANCELLED
POINT-A-PITRE	UX 1034	CANCELLED
SARAJEVO	OS 412	CANCELLED
LIMA	AF 2298	CANCELLED
ROME	KM 479	CANCELLED

'What happened . . . Why are they all cancelled?'

He steps back, obviously puzzled.

'You . . . you haven't heard?'

'No . . .'

'The eruption, the volcano?'

'The volcano, what volcano?'

'Ashes everywhere in the sky. They don't even know how long it's going to last! Days, weeks, maybe months! It's crazy!'

I look up at the sky: not a cloud. The guy is nuts.

'They are miniscule, invisible, no plane has been tested for this! And now, can you believe it! I live in Hong Kong! My wife, job, kids, what am I going to do? Only one suitcase, I can't stay! My office! The Chinese! I'm going to be fired!'

He notices an employee, runs up to him. The hall is teeming. Shouting. An agent is almost slapped. Our mother is on her deathbed. You can't leave us like this! You have to do something! A young girl grabs me.

'*Could you . . .*'

No, you have to let me go, everything I touch, the smallest thing, your hands, moreover, they shouldn't, yes, I assure you. The girl begs me with her look, all this panic, this noise, *all cancelled*, no one warned her, she can't bear it. A fight on my right, an old man has a spell. An increasingly dense crowd, what can I do, I'm not the volcano!

'Hallelujah!'

That voice in the middle of the disaster. I look at him, amazed. He grabs me, pulls me away.

'My queen, dance with me! Come celebrate with me, the Curtain is Rising!'

'Liam, please, let me go.'

More joyful than ever, he spins me around.

'The day of the Great Assembly has arrived, there is no longer any reason to be afraid. The birds will fly free from now on! Come on, let's dance! She will no longer scratch the ground with her nails until she bleeds.'

'Liam, it's only a volcano, the ashes of a volcano . . . '

He laughs even more.

'My queen, it's the Censor who invented that! The collapse of the Ten Destinations is happening, finally the Letters are going to disaccumulate! Dance, my queen, yes, and be at peace! Thanks to you, the order of Tourism is forever erased! The flow no longer exists! All fear gone! Where do you want them to expel us? Which land?'

'Liam, please, you're hurting me.'

But he holds me even tighter.

'Liam . . . '

He's no longer listening to me; I'm trying to fight him off when three security guards grab him, forcing him to let me go. One of them turns to me.

'Are you OK?'

'I . . . yes . . . thank you.'

He sighs.

'What a shitty day! OK, here we go, we'll take him away!'

In shock, I watch Liam being dragged away, then suddenly, with two violent movements of his shoulders, he frees himself. Stunned, the three guards don't react quickly enough. Like a madman Liam lunges at me. I try to avoid him by throwing myself backward, but he grabs me, shaking me furiously.

'My queen, we have won! The Censors are dead! Dead, do you hear?'

My heart is exploding. I stagger. People are all around me. A hand reaches out. Are you OK? My heart, the emotion, that is, everything is so sudden, they have to let me go, Vlad dead, you know, and Luc who is waiting for me, no, don't touch me, my hand, are you sure you're OK, yes, no, the sun is still so high, the heat so crushing, breathe, there, calmly, no, I can't, Vlad, my little sister, my little girl, dead because of me, to swerve at that speed, as if it were possible!

'Miss?'

I hurt so much all of a sudden, I'm running as fast as I can, but . . . Bang! Windshield, my shouts, breaking apart, my head, my father, my mother who greet me near the rose bushes, slope, oh so soft, I get up somewhere, hey, Luc is approaching, a rose in his hand.

'I've been looking for you everywhere.'

Something is dissolving, the sky? Such dense light, my parents, the slope to the fence, I remember the fence, the new owner who installed it when they died.

'Miss?'

And now this crowd looking at me, Marc, his face, defeated, leaning into my ear, our little girl who is no longer, my coma . . .

'I sold the house.'

Sold it—why? He turns around, walks away. No, he can't leave me like that, but, when I try to get up, impossible to move at all.

'Here, calm down, breathe slowly . . .'

Because I tell you that no one, ever, will be able to pardon me.

'Miss!'

No one, while I am flying higher and higher, leaving you all.

'Come on, Maude!'

That name . . . the breach that it opens in me.

'Come on, please, I've found something!'

She's leaning over, good God, why aren't you reacting, you, Vlad, you, Josias, you, Luc?! I turn my head to the left, I turn my head to the right, but nothing, no, no one at the very moment when the car at full speed crashes.

The ashes, spreading over the world.

Then, into the black infinity of things, I fall, bringing my existence in my wake, dreams of the airport where I've been walking for so long, when the melody of their laughter freezes me. I stare at them, stupefied. Let everything slip because of me, let everything collapse, but not them, no! Except, one of them weighs so much, agonized, I beg her not to let go of me, promise her my bed, my toys, everything! The little sister whom I loved so much and whom I wasn't able to . . . not able . . . whereas the other, sitting in the back seat of the car just when, right after the curve to my horror I discover that object in the middle of the road; the other, the little girl I loved with all my heart, as the car hit the edge full force, and, above the well, only with the strength of my hand, I tried desperately to hold her, until that terrible cry while the car was in the air and her little body, at the bottom of a well, thump! My little daughter, my sister, though, with all my strength, I don't push them, I don't kill them, insane night of the world, the fall that never ends, crazy with pain, all of us, travellers of the world, so bent over now, we are wavering, we are falling! That shouting we did then, the snow I removed by the shovelful so the entrance would be clear, while below, way down below, I hear the thump! of their little bodies, a thump! that pulverizes me and only a huge love will be able to repair me.

Only a huge love.

'Come on, Maude, come on, we've found something!'

This sorrow in me, this darkness it has created and into which I have been falling for so long. Isn't it finally time? It feels like an eternity that I've been dying for having killed them.

'Maude, come on!'

Run towards them. Don't resist any more.

'Look!'

Then, I lean over and for the first time I can see a bit of light (is that what they wanted to show me?), a tiny bit that, as I continue to stare at it, grows until it dazzles me. I'm eight years old. My little sister is dead. I've just learnt the news. Is it day? Is it night? I don't move. I don't cry. The days go by. In our room, I make her little bed, clean her Barbie castle from top to bottom. But nothing works, she doesn't come back.

The years go by, only the sight of snow sometimes moves me. That's how I grow up. In our room, the death room which, as the days go by, becomes mine.

Marc appears, we get married. But I am locked up in myself. Locked up behind windows where I feel nothing. Then, the miracle happens, I get pregnant and all my joy returns. Because it will be a little girl, I'm sure of it. A little girl whom I will name Élodie, like my sister, and who will repair everything. Console everything.

Soon, the little girl turns three. I exist only for her. Marc, exhausted, announces that he's leaving me. Without answering him, I get Élodie to take her out for a drive.

As I'm starting the car, Marc begs me to stay. For once we have an afternoon free together. We could try to talk.

Something in me hesitates. Something that begs me to stop being so hard. Except, in the car, Élodie is getting impatient and I hear myself answer: 'Tomorrow, if you want.'

Just as I'm turning onto the road, I see him, his face sad, gesturing in the rear-view mirror. But, in the back, Élodie is so joyful. I was right not to give in. Isn't she my life's breath? She, the light of my life? At the end of the straight road, a curve.

'Miss?'

Oh, but how is it possible? And all these travellers who are calling me and have their faces, as if, for ever, they had waited for me in this airport dream.

Then, knocking over the tree trunk, knocking over the well, I rush towards them, I kiss their little hands, I caress their hair, and everything, again, melts away.

'Miss?'

I open my eyes.

'Maude, my name is Maude.'

'That's good, Maude, breathe . . . You passed out. Sit up. There, like that . . . Would you like some water?'

I shake my head. I get up.

Alone in the hall. Alone facing the multitudes. In the heart of the letters 'Cancelled', she walks. At the centre of their fire.

Outside, billions of ashes are flying. Everywhere letters are glittering. In each one of them she dances, she leaps.

Under the radiant sky, she plants her steps. Letting the world appear. Recreating it.

I. The immensity of the world.

 EPILOGUE

Luc,

I'm leaving you this note which I'm taping to the walls all over the airport. You knew me as Anna, but my real name is Maude. Forgive me for running away from you. My memory has returned. I lost my little girl in a car accident, and my little sister, too, years ago. They were both named Élodie.

I wish I could have told you this in person, also told you that I love you, Luc, and that I am finally ready. Except, I can't find you. But you exist, I know it. You are there. A part of my life. And I'm waiting for you.

Maude

Acknowledgements

First of all, I wish to express my sincerest thanks to the entire staff at Roissy, and particularly to: Philippe Bargain, Carine Engrand, Jean-Paul Armangau, Mikael Lebris, Christophe Pauvel, the Emmaüs team, Father Francis Truptil, Father Baudoin Tournemine, Father Philippe Vanneste, Pierre Torres, Francois Heintz, Sebastien Farris, Sonia Gacic Blossier, Corinne Cousseau, Corinne Bokobza, as well as all the travellers . . .

I also want to thank from the bottom of my heart Isabelle Durand, who, with her boundless generosity, welcomed me every summer at her house in Louzelergue where I found the silence so essential to writing.

And finally, a huge thank you to Michele Gazier and Luc Lang for their very generous and loyal friendship and for reading my work; to Colo Tavernier, my mother, for her beautiful tenderness and her eagle eye; to my husband, Zavier, for his confidence and extreme love; to my daughter, Olivia, for all the happiness she brings me; and to Sabine Wespieser, my publisher, who has given me wings.